D0437538

Fantastic Creatures

AN ANTHOLOGY OF FANTASY AND SCIENCE FICTION

edited by ISAAC ASIMOV
Martin Greenberg
Charles Waugh

A GROLIER COMPANY

FRANKLIN WATTS
New York/London/Toronto/Sydney
1981

Library of Congress Cataloging in Publication Data

Main entry under title:

Fantastic creatures.

Contents: Introduction / by Isaac Asimov—The smallest dragonboy / by Ann McCaffrey—The Botticelli horror / by Lloyd Biggle, Jr.—[etc.]

1. Science fiction, American. 2. Children's stories, American. [1. Science fiction. 2. Short stories] I. Asimov, Isaac, 1920-   . II. Greenberg, Martin, 1918-   . III. Waugh, Charles.

PZ5F2147   [Fic]   81-10412
ISBN 0-531-04342-8   AACR2

B15310

Contents

INTRODUCTION
by Isaac Asimov
1

THE SMALLEST
DRAGONBOY
by Ann McCaffrey
5

THE BOTTICELLI
HORROR
by Lloyd Biggle, Jr.
20

KID CARDULA
by Jack Ritchie
62

THE MAN
FROM P.I.G.
by Harry Harrison
76

FLIGHT OVER XP-637
by Craig Sayre
106

THE BEES
FROM BORNEO
by Will H. Gray
117

THE ANGLERS
OF ARZ
by Roger Dee
131

THE GAME OF RAT
AND DRAGON
by Cordwainer Smith
140

INTRODUCTION
by Isaac Asimov

When civilization was young, what a fantastic planet we lived on. Strange creatures abounded wherever human beings looked. We've lost that wonder now, and it is hard for us even to imagine what it must have been like when even a short journey might bring us unbelievable sights.

Try to imagine . . .

Suppose you knew what cats, dogs, and various barnyard animals were like, as well as frogs, snakes, turtles, raccoons, and so on. And suppose you had never heard of anything else. Then suppose that, for the first time in your life, you saw an elephant, a giraffe, a camel, an ostrich, or even an armadillo.

Could you possibly have imagined these, or any of a hundred others, if you had never seen or heard of them?

Perhaps you might have imagined a bird as large as an ostrich, but would you have thought of its long neck or imagined it scudding across the plains on its two long legs, moving as quickly as a horse? Or if you had imagined an ox ten feet high at its shoulders, would you have thought of pulling its nose into a long snakelike appendage and making two giant fans of its ears?

It is no wonder that to early humans the earth seemed full of living wonders. It must have seemed that there was no limit to what might exist. Centaurs, sphinxes, harpies, mermaids, unicorns, winged horses, dragons, vampires, werewolves—almost anything that could entice, entrance, or affright was imagined.

But then, after 1500, the world began to shrink, and step-by-step the wonders retreated. Mermaids became sea cows; unicorns became rhinoceroses and narwhals; dragons became cobras.

Yet the world did not grow entirely tame, for even though imaginary creatures dwindled, there were new real discoveries. When the French naturalist Cuvier maintained that the animals on the American continents were just small and degenerate copies of those from the Old World, Thomas Jefferson had a moose stuffed and sent to him. Cuvier had to admit that no old-world deer could match that.

When Australia was explored, zoologists nearly went mad with wonder as whole new classes of animals—from the great red kangaroo on down—were revealed. They wouldn't believe the duckbill platypus really existed when a skin was sent to them. They thought it was a practical joke, that portions of skins of several creatures had been deftly stitched together.

Even older portions of the world had their surprises. As late as 1900, Europeans first spotted deep in the forests of Africa a new large mammal, a shy creature called the okapi—a shorter-necked relative of the giraffe with tentative zebralike stripes on its hindquarters.

The sea could hide quite a bit. The giant squid was finally discovered. It was not quite as big as the legendary kraken, but it was large enough to fight desperately for its life against the sperm whale. In the 1930s an odd fish that inhabited the middle depths was discovered. This discovery was not unusual except that the fish belonged to a group of sea creatures that were ancestors to land vertebrates (like ourselves) and were thought to have been extinct since the time of the dinosaur!

We can't help but dream of still more discoveries. Sea serpents slither in our imaginations; we even look for one in the tame and constricted waters of the Scottish Loch Ness. The Yeti (or Abominable Snowman) furtively makes its way up the slopes of Mount Everest, and Sasquatch (or Big Foot) hides from us in the forests of the American Northwest.

We can't even let go of the creatures we feared and loved in ancient days. The mermaids still sit on the rocks, combing their sea-green hair; centaurs still gallop through the woods while Pegasus wheels and soars up into the clouds; the dank forests of Eastern Europe still echo from the howl of the werewolf while the vast cities of the Western world lie prey to the skulking vampire.

Well, why not? Surely we can have the best of both worlds. Reality may be all about us, but we can nevertheless suspend disbelief and read tales, even today, that return us to fantasy.

In fact, by extending sober reality, we can spin new fantasies that the ancients never dreamed of.

The ancients knew only one world, and though it seemed big and fearsome and unknown, it remained only one. We now know that there are other worlds circling the sun, and in the last few centuries imaginative writers have filled every one of them with strange creatures of fancy. They have been the very stuff of science fiction.

But then in the last couple of decades, fantasy withered again before the awesomeness of stark reality. There are today twelve sets of human footprints on the moon, and objects made by human hands have rested upon the rocky surfaces of Mars and Venus. Human-made space probes, hooked to human eyes, have shown us the scarred surfaces of the planet Mercury and of satellites such as Phobos, Ganymede, Callisto, Dione, Rhea, and Mimas. They have shown us the smooth icy cover of Europa and Enceladus, the live volcanoes of Io, the thick, smoggy atmosphere of Titan, the monstrous Earth-sized storms in the writhing atmospheres of Jupiter and Saturn, and the amazing and unexpected complexity of the structure of Saturn's rings.

All this was undreamed of when wondering eyes, unaided by technology, swept the night sky and connected the stars to form figures of animals and heroes. But all that has been revealed is inanimate. The strange life dreamed of by science fiction writers has retreated as did the strange life once dreamed of by folktale constructors.

Where are the underground intelligences of the moon? Where are the wise and indomitable canal builders of Mars, wringing a despairing life out of a drying and dying world? Where is the rich, rank life belonging to the swamps and seas of wet and cloudy Venus?

Gone, all gone!

Well, it doesn't matter. We can cling as stubbornly to the old dreams of life in the solar system as we do to the monsters that peopled the Greek myths and the medieval European folktales.

Besides, there is the still farther beyond. Our own solar system is but one small family of worlds, and within that there is certainly one richly inhabited member—Earth. But our solar system is only one of a couple hundred billion in our galaxy alone, and there are a hundred billion other galaxies—all kinds of galaxies containing all kinds of stars circled by all kinds of planets bearing on them (surely!) all kinds of amazing creatures.

We can't reach those planets yet, but we can imagine them. And we can imagine them more elaborately and better than the ancients ever could—not because we're smarter than they were, but because we now have a wider experience with a greater variety of reality than they ever had the chance to have.

So here is a book of fantastic creatures as old as primitive human dreams and as new as the next century's headlines, as familiar as folktales yet as strange as science fiction—and all for your pleasure.

THE SMALLEST DRAGONBOY
by Ann McCaffrey

*Many societies have rites of passage in which
adolescents must complete certain ceremonial
tasks before being considered adults or being
allowed to assume adult responsibilities. On
the strange world of Pern, for example, a
young man cannot become a full-fledged
warrior—a dragonrider—unless he is chosen
from among many boys by one of Pern's
telepathic dragons. But sometimes, even getting
the chance to be chosen can be difficult.*

Although Keevan lengthened his walking stride as far as his
legs would stretch, he couldn't quite keep up with the other
candidates. He knew he would be teased again.

Just as he knew many other things that his foster mother
told him he ought not to know, Keevan knew that Beterli, the
most senior of the boys, set that spanking pace just to embarrass him, the smallest dragonboy. Keevan would arrive, tail
fork-end of the group, breathless, chest heaving, and maybe get
a stern look from the instructing wingsecond.

Dragonriders, even if they were still only hopeful candidates
for the glowing eggs which were hardening on the hot sands of
the Hatching Ground cavern, were expected to be punctual and
prepared. Sloth was not tolerated by the Weyrleader of Benden
Weyr. A good record was especially important now. It was very
near hatching time, when the baby dragons would crack their
mottled shells, and stagger forth to choose their lifetime com-
panions. The very thought of that glorious moment made
Keevan's breath catch in his throat. To be chosen—to be a
dragonrider! To sit astride the neck of a winged beast with
jeweled eyes: to be his friend, in telepathic communion with
him for life; to be his companion in good times and fighting
extremes; to fly effortlessly over the lands of Pern! Or, thrillingly,

between to any point anywhere on the world! Flying *between* was done on dragonback or not at all, and it was dangerous.

Keevan glanced upward, past the black mouths of the weyr caves in which grown dragons and their chosen riders lived, toward the Star Stones that crowned the ridge of the old volcano that was Benden Weyr. On the height, the blue watch dragon, his rider mounted on his neck, stretched the great transparent pinions that carried him on the winds of Pern to fight the evil Thread that fell at certain times from the skies. The many-faceted rainbow jewels of his eyes glistened fleetingly in the greeny sun. He folded his great wings to his back, and the watch pair resumed their statuelike pose of alertness.

Then the enticing view was obscured as Keevan passed into the Hatching Ground cavern. The sands underfoot were hot, even through heavy wher-hide boots. How the bootmaker had protested having to sew so small! Keevan was forced to wonder why being small was reprehensible. People were always calling him "babe" and shooing him away as being "too small" or "too young" for this or that. Keevan was constantly working, twice as hard as any other boy his age, to prove himself capable. What if his muscles weren't as big as Beterli's? They were just as hard. And if he couldn't overpower anyone in a wrestling match, he could outdistance everyone in a footrace.

"Maybe if you run fast enough," Beterli had jeered on the occasion when Keevan had been goaded to boast of his swiftness, "you could catch a dragon. That's the only way you'll make a dragonrider!"

"You just wait and see, Beterli, you just wait," Keevan had replied. He would have liked to wipe the contemptuous smile from Beterli's face, but the guy didn't fight fair even when a wingsecond was watching. "No one knows what Impresses a dragon!"

"They've got to be able to *find* you first, babe!"

Yes, being the smallest candidate was not an enviable position. It was therefore imperative that Keevan Impress a dragon in his first hatching. That would wipe the smile off every face in the cavern and accord him the respect due any dragonrider, even the smallest one.

Besides, no one knew exactly what Impressed the baby dragons as they struggled from their shells in search of their lifetime partners.

"I like to believe that dragons see into a man's heart," Keevan's foster mother, Mende, told him. "If they find goodness, honesty, a flexible mind, patience, courage—and you've got that in quantity, dear Keevan—that's what dragons look for. I've seen many a well-grown lad left standing on the sands, Hatching Day, in favor of someone not so strong or tall or handsome. And if my memory serves me"—which it usually did: Mende knew every word of every Harper's tale worth telling, although Keevan did not interrupt her to say so—"I don't believe that F'lar, our Weyrleader, was all that tall when bronze Mnementh chose him. And Mnementh was the only bronze dragon of that hatching."

Dreams of Impressing a bronze were beyond Keevan's boldest reflections, although that goal dominated the thoughts of every other hopeful candidate. Green dragons were small and fast and more numerous. There was more prestige to Impressing a blue or brown than a green. Being practical, Keevan seldom dreamed as high as a big fighting brown, like Canth, F'nor's fine fellow, the biggest brown on all Pern. But to fly a bronze? Bronzes were almost as big as the queen, and only they took the air when a queen flew at mating time. A bronze rider could aspire to become Weyrleader! Well, Keevan would console himself, brown riders could aspire to become wingseconds, and that wasn't bad. He'd even settle for a green dragon: they were small, but so was he. No matter! He simply had to Impress a dragon his first time in the Hatching Ground. Then no one in the Weyr would taunt him anymore for being so small.

Shells, Keevan thought now, but the sands are hot!

"Impression time is imminent, candidates," the wingsecond was saying as everyone crowded respectfully close to him. "See the extent of the striations on this promising egg." The stretch marks *were* larger than yesterday.

Everyone leaned forward and nodded thoughtfully. That particular egg was the one Beterli had marked as his own, and no other candidate dared, on pain of being beaten by Beterli at his first opportunity, to approach it. The egg was marked by a large yellowish splotch in the shape of a dragon backwinging to land, talons outstretched to grasp rock. Everyone knew that bronze eggs bore distinctive markings. And naturally, Beterli, who'd been presented at eight Impressions already and was the biggest of the candidates, had chosen it.

"I'd say that the great opening day is almost upon us," the wingsecond went on, and then his face assumed a grave expression. "As we well know, there are only forty eggs and seventy-two candidates. Some of you may be disappointed on the great day. That doesn't necessarily mean you aren't dragonrider material, just that *the* dragon for you hasn't been shelled. You'll have other hatchings, and it's no disgrace to be left behind an Impression or two. Or more."

Keevan was positive that the wingsecond's eyes rested on Beterli, who'd been stood off at so many Impressions already. Keevan tried to squinch down so the wingsecond wouldn't notice him. Keevan had been reminded too often that he was eligible to be a candidate by one day only. He, of all the hopefuls, was most likely to be left standing on the great day. One more reason why he simply had to Impress at his first hatching.

"Now move about among the eggs," the wingsecond said. "Touch them. We don't know that it does any good, but it certainly doesn't do any harm."

Some of the boys laughed nervously, but everyone immediately began to circulate among the eggs. Beterli stepped up officiously to "his" egg, daring anyone to come near it. Keevan smiled, because he had already touched it—every inspection day, when the others were leaving the Hatching Ground and no one could see him crouch to stroke it.

Keevan had an egg he concentrated on, too, one drawn slightly to the far side of the others. The shell had a soft greenish-blue tinge with a faint creamy swirl design. The consensus was that this egg contained a mere green, so Keevan was rarely bothered by rivals. He was somewhat perturbed then to see Beterli wandering over to him.

"I don't know why you're allowed in this Impression, Keevan. There are enough of us without a babe," Beterli said, shaking his head.

"I'm of age." Keevan kept his voice level, telling himself not to be bothered by mere words.

"Yah!" Beterli made a show of standing on his toetips. "You can't even see over an egg; Hatching Day, you better get in front or the dragons won't see you at all. 'Course, you could get run down that way in the mad scramble. Oh, I forget, you can run fast, can't you?"

"You'd better make sure a dragon sees *you*, this time, Beterli," Keevan replied. "You're almost overage, aren't you?"

Beterli flushed and took a step forward, hand half-raised. Keevan stood his ground, but if Beterli advanced one more step, he would call the wingsecond. No one fought on the Hatching Ground. Surely Beterli knew that much.

Fortunately, at that moment, the wingsecond called the boys together and led them from the Hatching Ground to start on evening chores. There were "glows" to be replenished in the main kitchen caverns and sleeping cubicles, the major hallways, and the queen's apartment. Firestone sacks had to be filled against Thread attack, and black rock brought to the kitchen hearths. The boys fell to their chores, tantalized by the odors of roasting meat. The population of the Weyr began to assemble for the evening meal, and the dragonriders came in from the Feeding Ground on their sweep checks.

It was the time of day Keevan liked best: once the chores were done but before dinner was served, a fellow could often get close enough to the dragonriders to hear their talk. Tonight, Keevan's father, K'last, was at the main dragonrider table. It puzzled Keevan how his father, a brown rider and a tall man, could *be* his father—because he, Keevan, was so small. It obviously puzzled K'last, too, when he deigned to notice his small son: "In a few more Turns, you'll be as tall as I am—or taller!"

K'last was pouring Benden wine all around the table. The dragonriders were relaxing. There'd be no Thread attack for three more days, and they'd be in the mood to tell tall tales, better than Harper yarns, about impossible maneuvers they'd done a-dragonback. When Thread attack was closer, their talk would change to a discussion of tactics of evasion, of going *between*, how long to suspend there until the burning but fragile Thread would freeze and crack and fall harmlessly off dragon and man. They would dispute the exact moment to feed fire-stone to the dragon so he'd have the best flame ready to sear Thread midair and render it harmless to ground—and man—below. There was such a lot to know and understand about being a dragonrider that sometimes Keevan was overwhelmed. How would he ever be able to remember everything he ought to know at the right moment? He couldn't dare ask such a question; this would only have given additional weight to the notion that he was too young yet to be a dragonrider.

"Having older candidates makes good sense," L'vel was saying, as Keevan settled down near the table. "Why waste four to five years of a dragon's fighting prime until his rider grows up enough to stand the rigors?" L'vel had Impressed a blue of Ramoth's first clutch. Most of the candidates thought L'vel was marvelous because he spoke up in front of the older riders, who awed them. "That was well enough in the Interval when you didn't need to mount the full Weyr complement to fight Thread. But not now. Not with more eligible candidates than ever. Let the babes wait."

"Any boy who is over twelve Turns has the right to stand in the Hatching Ground," K'last replied, a slight smile on his face. He never argued or got angry. Keevan wished he were more like his father. And oh, how he wished he were a brown rider! "Only a dragon—each particular dragon—knows what he wants in a rider. We certainly can't tell. Time and again the theorists," K'last's smile deepened as his eyes swept those at the table, "are surprised by dragon choice. *They* never seem to make mistakes, however."

"Now, K'last, just look at the roster this Impression. Seventy-two boys and only forty eggs. Drop off the twelve youngest, and there's still a good field for the hatchlings to choose from. Shells! There are a couple of weyrlings unable to see over a wher egg much less a dragon! And years before they can ride Thread."

"True enough, but the Weyr is scarcely under fighting strength, and if the youngest Impress, they'll be old enough to fight when the oldest of our current dragons go *between* from senility."

"Half the Weyr-bred lads have already been through several

·Impressions," one of the bronze riders said then. "I'd say drop some of *them* off this time. Give the untried a chance."

"There's nothing wrong in presenting a clutch with as wide a choice as possible," said the Weyrleader, who had joined the table with Lessa, the Weyrwoman.

"Has there ever been a case," she said, smiling in her odd way at the riders, "where a hatchling didn't choose?"

Her suggestion was almost heretical and drew astonished gasps from everyone, including the boys.

F'lar laughed. "You say the most outrageous things, Lessa."

"Well, *has* there ever been a case where a dragon didn't choose?"

"Can't say as I recall one," K'last replied.

"Then we continue in this tradition," Lessa said firmly, as if that ended the matter.

But it didn't. The argument ranged from one table to the other all through dinner, with some favoring a weeding out of the candidates to the most likely, lopping off those who were very young or who had had multiple opportunities to Impress. All the candidates were in a swivet, though such a departure from tradition would be to the advantage of many. As the evening progressed, more riders were favoring eliminating the youngest and those who'd passed four or more Impressions unchosen. Keevan felt he could bear such a dictum only if Beterli were also eliminated. But this seemed less likely than that Keevan would be turfed out, since the Weyr's need was for fighting dragons and riders.

By the time the evening meal was over, no decision had been reached, although the Weyrleader had promised to give the matter due consideration.

He might have slept on the problem, but few of the candidates did. Tempers were uncertain in the sleeping caverns next morning as the boys were routed out of their beds to carry water and black rock and cover the "glows." Twice Mende had to call Keevan to order for clumsiness.

"Whatever is the matter with you, boy?" she demanded in exasperation when he tipped black rock short of the bin and sooted up the hearth.

"They're going to keep me from this Impression."

"What?" Mende stared at him. "Who?"

"You heard them talking at dinner last night. They're going to turf the babes from the hatching."

Mende regarded him a moment longer before touching his arm gently. "There's lots of talk around a supper table, Keevan. And it cools as soon as the supper. I've heard the same nonsense before every hatching, but nothing is ever changed."

"There's always a first time," Keevan answered, copying one of her own phrases.

"That'll be enough of that, Keevan. Finish your job. If the clutch does hatch today, we'll need full rock bins for the feast, and you won't be around to do the filling. All my fosterlings make dragonriders."

"The first time?" Keevan was bold enough to ask as he scooted off with the rockbarrow.

Perhaps, Keevan thought later, if he hadn't been on that chore just when Beterli was also fetching black rock, things might have turned out differently. But he had dutifully trundled the barrow to the outdoor bunker for another load just as Beterli arrived on a similar errand.

"Heard the news, babe?" Beterli asked. He was grinning from ear to ear, and he put an unnecessary emphasis on the final insulting word.

"The eggs are cracking?" Keevan all but dropped the loaded shovel. Several anxieties flicked through his mind then: he was black with rock dust—would he have time to wash before donning the white tunic of candidacy? And if the eggs were hatching, why hadn't the candidates been recalled by the wingsecond?

"Naw! Guess again!" Beterli was much too pleased with himself.

With a sinking heart, Keevan knew what the news must be, and he could only stare with intense desolation at the older boy.

"C'mon! Guess, babe!"

"I've no time for guessing games," Keevan managed to say with indifference. He began to shovel black rock into the barrow as fast as he could.

"I said, guess." Beterli grabbed the shovel.

"And I said I have no time for guessing games."

Beterli wrenched the shovel from Keevan's hands. "Guess!"

"I'll have that shovel back, Beterli." Keevan straightened up, but he didn't come to Beterli's bulky shoulder. From somewhere, other boys appeared, some with barrows, some mysteriously alerted to the prospect of a confrontation among their numbers.

"Babes don't give orders to candidates around here, babe!"

Someone sniggered and Keevan, incredulous, knew that he must've been dropped from the candidacy.

He yanked the shovel from Beterli's loosened grasp. Snarling, the older boy tried to regain possession, but Keevan clung with all his strength to the handle, dragged back and forth as the stronger boy jerked the shovel about.

With a sudden, unexpected movement, Beterli rammed the handle into Keevan's chest, knocking him over the barrow handles. Keevan felt a sharp, painful jab behind his left ear, an unbearable pain in his left shin, and then a painless nothingness.

Mende's angry voice roused him, and startled, he tried to throw back the covers, thinking he'd overslept. But he couldn't move, so firmly was he tucked into his bed. And then the constriction of a bandage on his head and the dull sickishness in his leg brought back recent occurrences.

"Hatching?" he cried.

"No, lovey," Mende said in a kind voice. Her hand was cool and gentle on his forehead. "Though there's some as won't be at any hatching again." Her voice took on a stern edge.

Keevan looked beyond her to see the Weyrwoman, who was frowning with irritation.

"Keevan, will you tell me what occurred at the black-rock bunker?" asked Lessa in an even voice.

He remembered Beterli now and the quarrel over the shovel and . . . what had Mende said about some not being at any hatching? Much as he hated Beterli, he couldn't bring himself to tattle on Beterli and force him out of candidacy.

"Come, lad," and a note of impatience crept into the Weyrwoman's voice. "I merely want to know what happened from you, too. Mende said she sent you for black rock. Beterli—and every Weyrling in the cavern—seems to have been on the same errand. What happened?"

"Beterli took my shovel. I hadn't finished with it."

"There's more than one shovel. What did he *say* to you?"

"He'd heard the news."

"What news?" The Weyrwoman was suddenly amused.

"That . . . that . . . there'd been changes."

"Is that what he said?"

"Not exactly."

"What did he say? C'mon, lad, I've heard from everyone else, you know."

"He said for me to guess the news."

"And you fell for that old gag?" The Weyrwoman's irritation returned.

"Consider all the talk last night at supper, Lessa," Mende said. "Of course the boy would think he'd been eliminated."

"In effect, he is, with a broken skull and leg." Lessa touched his arm in a rare gesture of sympathy. "Be that as it may, Keevan, you'll have other Impressions. Beterli will not. There are certain rules that must be observed by all candidates, and his conduct proves him unacceptable to the Weyr."

She smiled at Mende and then left.

"I'm still a candidate?" Keevan asked urgently.

"Well, you are and you aren't, lovey," his foster mother said. "Is the numbweed working?" she asked, and when he nodded, she said, "You just rest. I'll bring you some nice broth."

At any other time in his life, Keevan would have relished such cosseting, but now he just lay there worrying. Beterli had been dismissed. Would the others think it was his fault? But everyone was there! Beterli provoked that fight. His worry increased, because although he heard excited comings and goings in the passageway, no one tweaked back the curtain across the sleeping alcove he shared with five other boys. Surely one of them would have to come in sometime. No, they were all avoiding him. And something else was wrong. Only he didn't know what.

Mende returned with broth and beachberry bread.

"Why doesn't anyone come see me, Mende? I haven't done anything wrong, have I? I didn't ask to have Beterli turfed out."

Mende soothed him, saying everyone was busy with noontime chores and no one was angry with him. They were giving him a chance to rest in quiet. The numbweed made him drowsy, and her words were fair enough. He permitted his fears to dissipate. Until he heard a hum. Actually, he felt it first, in the broken shin bone and his sore head. The hum began to grow. Two things registered suddenly in Keevan's groggy mind: the only white candidate's robe still on the pegs in the chamber was his; and the dragons hummed when a clutch was being laid or being hatched. Impression! And he was flat abed.

Bitter, bitter disappointment turned the warm broth sour in his belly. Even the small voice telling him that he'd have other opportunities failed to alleviate his crushing depression. *This* was the Impression that mattered! This was his chance to show *everyone*, from Mende to K'last to L'vel and even the Weyrleader that he, Keevan, was worthy of being a dragonrider.

He twisted in bed, fighting against the tears that threatened to choke him. Dragonmen don't cry! Dragonmen learn to live with pain.

Pain? The leg didn't actually pain him as he rolled about on his bedding. His head felt sort of stiff from the tightness of the bandage. He sat up, an effort in itself since the numbweed made exertion difficult. He touched the splinted leg; the knee was unhampered. He had no feeling in his bone, really. He swung himself carefully to the side of his bed and stood slowly. The room wanted to swim about him. He closed his eyes, which made the dizziness worse, and he had to clutch the wall.

Gingerly, he took a step. The broken leg dragged. It hurt in spite of the numbweed, but what was pain to a dragonman?

No one had said he couldn't go to the Impression. "You are and you aren't," were Mende's exact words.

Clinging to the wall, he jerked off his bedshirt. Stretching his arm to the utmost, he jerked his white candidate's tunic from the peg. Jamming first one arm and then the other into the holes, he pulled it over his head. Too bad about the belt. He couldn't wait. He hobbled to the door, hung on to the curtain to steady himself. The weight on his leg was unwieldy. He wouldn't get very far without something to lean on. Down by the bathing pool was one of the long crook-necked poles used to retrieve clothes from the hot washing troughs. But it was down there, and he was on the level above. And there was no one nearby to come to his aid: everyone would be in the Hatching Ground right now, eagerly waiting for the first egg to crack.

The humming increased in volume and tempo, an urgency to which Keevan responded, knowing that his time was all too limited if he was to join the ranks of the hopeful boys standing around the cracking eggs. But if he hurried down the ramp, he'd fall flat on his face.

He could, of course, go flat on his rear end, the way crawling children did. He sat down, sending a jarring stab of pain through his leg and up to the wound on the back of his head. Gritting his teeth and blinking away tears, Keevan scrabbled down the ramp. He had to wait a moment at the bottom to catch his breath. He got to one knee, the injured leg straight out in front of him. Somehow, he managed to push himself erect, though the room seemed about to tip over his ears. It wasn't far to the crooked stick, but it seemed an age before he had it in his hand.

Then the humming stopped!

Keevan cried out and began to hobble frantically across the cavern, out to the bowl of the Weyr. Never had the distance between living caverns and the Hatching Ground seemed so great. Never had the Weyr been so breathlessly silent. It was as if the multitude of people and dragons watching the hatching held every breath in suspense. Not even the wind muttered down the steep sides of the bowl. The only sounds to break the stillness were Keevan's ragged gasps and the thump-thud of his stick on the hard-packed ground. Sometimes he had to hop twice on his good leg to maintain his balance. Twice he fell into the sand and had to pull himself up on the stick, his white tunic no longer spotless. Once he jarred himself so badly he couldn't get up immediately.

Then he heard the first exhalation of the crowd, the oohs, the muted cheer, the susurrus of excited whispers. An egg had cracked, and the dragon had chosen his rider. Desperation increased Keevan's hobble. Would he never reach the arching mouth of the Hatching Ground?

Another cheer and an excited spate of applause spurred Keevan to greater effort. If he didn't get there in moments, there'd be no unpaired hatchling left. Then he was actually staggering into the Hatching Ground, the sands hot on his bare feet.

No one noticed his entrance or his halting progress. And Keevan could see nothing but the backs of the white-robed candidates, seventy of them ringing the area around the eggs. Then one side would surge forward or back and there'd be a cheer. Another dragon had been Impressed. Suddenly a large gap appeared in the white human wall, and Keevan had his first sight of the eggs. There didn't seem to be *any* left uncracked, and he could see the lucky boys standing beside wobble-legged dragons. He could hear the unmistakable plaintive crooning of hatchlings and their squawks of protest as they'd fall awkwardly in the sand.

Suddenly he wished that he hadn't left his bed, that he'd stayed away from the Hatching Ground. Now everyone would see his ignominious failure. So he scrambled as desperately to reach the shadowy walls of the Hatching Ground as he had struggled to cross the bowl. He mustn't be seen.

He didn't notice, therefore, that the shifting group of boys remaining had begun to drift in his direction. The hard pace he had set himself and his cruel disappointment took their double toll of Keevan. He tripped and collapsed sobbing to the warm sands. He didn't see the consternation in the watching Weyrfolk above the Hatching Ground, nor did he hear the excited whispers of speculation. He didn't know that the Weyrleader and Weyrwoman had dropped to the arena and were making their way toward the knot of boys slowly moving in the direction of the entrance.

"Never seen anything like it," the Weyrleader was saying. "Only thirty-nine riders chosen. And the bronze trying to leave the Hatching Ground without making Impression."

"A case in point of what I said last night," the Weyrwoman

replied, "where a hatchling makes no choice because the right boy isn't there."

"There's only Beterli and K'last's young one missing. And there's a full wing of likely boys to choose from . . ."

"None acceptable, apparently. Where is the creature going? He's not heading for the entrance after all. Oh, what have we there, in the shadows?"

Keevan heard with dismay the sound of voices nearing him. He tried to burrow into the sand. The mere thought of how he would be teased and taunted now was unbearable.

Don't worry! Please don't worry! The thought was urgent, but not his own.

Someone kicked sand over Keevan and butted roughly against him.

"Go away. Leave me alone!" he cried.

Why? was the injured-sounding question inserted into his mind. There was no voice, no tone, but the question was there, perfectly clear, in his head.

Incredulous, Keevan lifted his head and stared into the glowing jeweled eyes of a small bronze dragon. His wings were wet, the tips drooping in the sand. And he sagged in the middle on his unsteady legs, although he was making a great effort to keep erect.

Keevan dragged himself to his knees, oblivious of the pain in his leg. He wasn't even aware that he was ringed by the boys passed over, while thirty-one pairs of resentful eyes watched him Impress the dragon. The Weyrmen looked on, amused and surprised at the draconic choice, which could not be forced. Could not be questioned. Could not be changed.

Why? asked the dragon again. *Don't you like me?* His eyes whirled with anxiety, and his tone was so piteous that Keevan staggered forward and threw his arms around the dragon's neck, stroking his eye ridges, patting the damp, soft hide, opening the fragile-looking wings to dry them, and wordlessly assuring the hatchling over and over again that he was the most perfect, most beautiful, most beloved dragon in the Weyr, in all the Weyrs of Pern.

"What's his name, K'van?" asked Lessa, smiling warmly at

the new dragonrider. K'van stared up at her for a long moment. Lessa would know as soon as he did. Lessa was the only person who could "receive" from all dragons, not only her own Ramoth. Then he gave her a radiant smile, recognizing the traditional shortening of his name that raised him forever to the rank of dragonrider.

My name is Heth, the dragon thought mildly, then hiccuped in sudden urgency. *I'm hungry.*

"Dragons are born hungry," said Lessa, laughing. "F'lar, give the boy a hand. He can barely manage his own legs, much less a dragon's."

K'van remembered his stick and drew himself up. "We'll be just fine, thank you."

"You may be the smallest dragonrider ever, young K'van," F'lar said, "but you're one of the bravest!"

And Heth agreed! Pride and joy so leaped in both chests that K'van wondered if his heart would burst right out of his body. He looped an arm around Heth's neck and the pair, the smallest dragonboy and the hatchling who wouldn't choose anybody else, walked out of the Hatching Ground together forever.

THE BOTTICELLI HORROR
by Lloyd Biggle, Jr.

*For those of you who may be aspiring movie
directors, here is a story that reads like a
science fiction film script. Indeed, it seems
to form a perfect bridge between the classic
monster films of the 1950s, such as* The Thing
and Them, *and the ecological films of the
1970s, such as* Silent Running *and* The China
Syndrome.

Even from a thousand feet the town of Gwinn Center, Kansas,
looked frightened.

The streets were deserted. The clumsy ground vehicles that
crept along the twisting black ribbon of roadway miles beyond
the town were headed south, running away. Stretched across the
rich green of the cultivated fields was a wavering line of dots.
As John Allen slanted his plane downward the dots enlarged and
became men who edged forward doggedly, holding weapons at
the ready.

The town was not completely abandoned. As Allen circled
to pick out a landing place he saw a man dart from one of the
commercial buildings, run at top speed along the center of a
street, and with a final, furtive glance over his shoulder, disappear into a house. None of this surprised Allen. The message
that had been plunked on his desk at Terran Customs an hour
and a half before was explanation enough. The lurking atmosphere of terror, the fleeing townspeople, the grim line of armed
men—Allen had expected all of that.

It was the tents that puzzled him.

They formed a square in a meadow near the edge of town,
a miniature village of flapping brown and green canvas. Allen's
message didn't account for the tents.

He circled again, spotted a police plane that was parked on one of the town's wider streets. A small group of men stood nearby in the shadow of a building. Allen completed his turn and pointed the plane downward.

Dr. Ralph Hilks lifted his nose from the scientific journal that had claimed his entire attention from the moment of their takeoff and peered down curiously. "Is this the place? Where is everyone?"

"Hiding, probably," Allen said. "Those that haven't already left."

"What are the tents?"

"I haven't any idea."

Hilks grunted. "Looks as if we've been handed a hot one," he said and returned to his reading.

Allen concentrated on the landing. They floated straight down and came to rest beside the police plane with a gentle thud.

Hilks closed his journal a second time. "Nice," he observed.

Allen cut the motor. "Thanks," he said dryly. "It has the new-type shocks."

They climbed out. The little group of men—there were four of them—had turned to watch them land. Not caring to waste time on formalities, Allen went to meet them.

"Allen is my name," he said. "Chief Customs Investigator. And this—" He paused until the pudgy, slow-moving scientist had caught up with him. "This is Dr. Hilks, our scientific consultant."

The men squared away for introductions. The tall one was Fred Corning, State Commissioner of Police. The young man in uniform was his aide, a Sergeant Darrow. The sturdy, deeply tanned individual with alert eyes and slow speech was Sheriff Townsend. The fourth man, old, wispy, with startlingly white, unruly hair and eyeglasses that could have been lifted from a museum, was Dr. Anderson, a medical doctor. All four of them were grim, and the horror that gripped the town had not left them unmarked, but at least they weren't frightened.

"You didn't waste any time getting here," the commissioner said. "We're glad of that."

"No," Allen said. "Let's not waste time now."

"I suppose you want to see the—ah—remains?"

"That's as good a place to start as any."

"This way," the commissioner said.

They moved off along the center of the street.

The house was one of a row of houses at the edge of town. It was small and tidy-looking, a white building with red shutters and window boxes full of flowers. The splashes of color should have given it a cheerful appearance, but in that town, on that day, nothing appeared cheerful.

The yard at the rear of the house was enclosed by a shoulder-high picket fence. They paused while the commissioner fussed with the fastener on the gate, and Dr. Hilks stood gaping at the row of houses.

The commissioner swung the gate open and turned to look at him. "See anything?"

"Chimneys!" Hilks said. "Every one of these dratted buildings has its own chimney. Think of it—a couple of hundred heating plants, and the town isn't large enough for one to function efficiently. The waste must be—"

The others moved through the gate and left him talking to himself.

At the rear of the yard a sheet lay loosely over unnatural contours. "We took photographs, of course," the commissioner said, "but it's so incredible—we wanted you to see—"

The four men each took a corner, raised the sheet carefully, and moved it away. Allen caught his breath and stepped back a pace.

"We left—things—just as they were," the commissioner said. "Except for the child that survived, of course. He was rushed—"

At Allen's feet lay the head of a blonde, blue-eyed child. She was no more than six, a young beauty who doubtless had already caused romantic palpitations in the hearts of her male playmates.

But no longer. The head was severed cleanly just below the chin. The eyes were wide open, and on the face was a haunting expression of indescribable horror. A few scraps of clothing lay where her body should have been.

A short distance away were other scraps of clothing and two shoes. Allen winced as he noticed that one shoe contained a foot. The other was empty. He circled to the other side, where two more shoes lay. Both were empty. Hilks was kneeling by the pathetic little head.

"No bleeding?" Hilks asked.

"No bleeding," Dr. Anderson said hoarsely. "If there had been, the other child—the one that survived—would have died. But the wounds were—cauterized, you might say, though I doubt that it's the right word. Anyway, there wasn't any bleeding."

Dr. Hilks bent close to the severed head. "You mean heat was applied—"

"I didn't say heat," Dr. Anderson said testily.

"We figure it happened like this," the commissioner said. "The three children were playing here in the yard. They were Sharon Brown, the eldest, and her little sister Ruth, who was three, and Johnnie Larkins, from next door. He's five. The mothers were in the house, and no one would have thought anything could possibly happen to the kids."

"The mothers didn't hear anything?" Allen asked.

The commissioner shook his head.

"Strange they wouldn't yell or scream or something."

"Perhaps they did. The carnival was making a powerful lot of noise, so the mothers didn't hear anything."

"Carnival?"

The commissioner nodded at the tents.

"Oh," Allen said, looking beyond the fence for the first time since he'd entered the yard. "So that's what it is."

"The kids were probably standing close together, playing something or maybe looking at something, and they didn't see the—see it—coming. When they did see it they tried to scatter, but it was too late. The thing dropped on them and pinned them down. Sharon was completely covered except for her head. Ruth was covered except for one foot. And Johnnie, maybe because he was the most active or maybe because he was standing apart a little, almost got away. His legs were covered, but only to his knees. And then—the thing ate them."

Allen shuddered in spite of himself. "*Ate* them? Bones and all?"

"That's the wrong word," Dr. Anderson said. "I would say —*absorbed* them."

"It seems to have absorbed most of their clothing, too," Allen said. "Also, Sharon's shoes."

The commissioner shook his head. "No. No shoes. Sharon wasn't wearing any, and it left the others' shoes. Well, this is what the mothers found when they came out. They're both in bad shape, and I doubt that Mrs. Brown will ever be the same again. We don't know yet whether Johnnie Larkins will recover. We don't know what the aftereffects might be when something like that eats part of you."

Allen turned to Hilks. "Any ideas?"

"I'd like to know a little more about this *thing*. Did anyone catch a glimpse of it?"

"Probably a couple of thousand people around here have seen it," the commissioner said. "Now we'll go talk to Bronsky."

"Who's Bronsky?" Allen asked.

"He's the guy that owned it."

They left Dr. Anderson at the scene of the tragedy to supervise whatever was to be done with the pathetic remains. The commissioner led the way through a rear gate and across the meadow to the tents.

Above the entrance a fluttering streamer read, JOLLY BROTHERS SHOWS. They entered, with Hilks mopping his perspiring face and complaining about the heat, Allen looking about alertly, and the others walking ahead in silence.

Allen turned his attention first to the strange apparatus that stood in the broad avenue between the tents. He saw miniature rocket ships, miniature planes, miniature ground cars, and devices too devious in appearance to identify, but he quickly puzzled out the fact that a carnival was a kind of traveling amusement park.

Hilks had paused to look at a poster featuring a row of

scantily clad young ladies. "*They* look cool," he muttered, mopping his face again.

Allen took his arm and pulled him along. "They're also of unmistakable terrestrial origin. We're looking for a monster from outer space."

"This place is something right out of the twentieth century," Hilks said. "If not the nineteenth. Ever see one before?"

"No, but I've seen stuff like this in amusement parks. I guess a carnival just moves it around."

Sheriff Townsend spoke over his shoulder. "This carnival has been coming here every year for as long as I can remember."

They passed a tent that bore the flaming title, EXOTIC WONDERS OF THE UNIVERSE. The illustrations were lavishly colored and immodestly exaggerated. A gigantic flower that Allen recognized as vaguely resembling a Venusian Meat-Eater was holding a struggling rodent in its fangs. A vine, also from Venus, was in hot pursuit of a frantic young lady it had presumably surprised in the act of dressing. The plants illustrated were all Venusian, Allen thought, though the poster mentioned lichens from Mars and a Luna Vacuum Flower.

"That isn't the place," the commissioner said. "There isn't anything in there but plants and rocks."

"I'd like to take a look," Allen said. He raised the tent flap. In the dim light he could see long rows of plastic display cases, each tagged with the bright yellow import permit of Terran Customs.

"I'll take another look later, but things seem to be in proper order," he said.

They moved on and stopped in front of the most startling picture Allen had ever seen. A girl arose genie-like from the yawning opening of an enormous shell. Her shapely body was—perhaps—human. Tentacles intertwined nervously where her hair should have been. Her hands were webbed claws, her facial expression the rigid, staring look of a lunatic, and her torso tapered away into the sinister darkness of the shell's interior.

"This is it," the commissioner said.

"*This?*" Allen echoed doubtfully.

"That's one of the things it did in the act."

Hilks had been staring intently at the poster. Suddenly he giggled. "Know what that looks like? There was an old painting by one of those early Italians. Da Vinci, maybe. Or Botticelli. I think it was Botticelli. It was called 'The Birth of Venus,' and it had a dame standing on a shell in just about that posture— except that the dame was human and not bad-looking. I wonder what happened to it. Maybe it went up with the old Louvre. I've seen reproductions of it. I may have one at home."

"I doubt that it has much bearing on our present problem," the commissioner said dryly.

Hilks slapped his thigh. "Allen! Some dratted artist has a fiendish sense of humor. I'll give you odds this *thing* comes from Venus. It'll have to. And the painting was called, 'The Birth of Venus.' From heavenly beauty to Earthly horror. Pretty good, eh?"

"If you don't mind—" the commissioner said.

They followed him into the tent. Allen caught a passing glimpse of a sign that read, "Elmer, the Giant Snail. The World's Greatest Mimic." There was more, but he didn't bother to read it. He figured that he was too late for the show.

Bronsky was a heavy-set man of medium height, with a high forehead that merged with the gleaming dome of his bald head. His eyes were piercing, angry. At the same time he seemed frightened.

"Elmer didn't do it!" he shouted.

"So you say," the commissioner said. "This is Chief-Inspector Allen. And Dr. Hilks. Tell them about it."

Bronsky eyed them sullenly.

"Do you have a photograph of Elmer?" Allen asked.

Bronsky nodded and disappeared through a curtain at the rear of the tent. Allen nudged Hilks, and they walked together toward the curtain. Behind it was a roped-off platform six feet high. On the platform was a shallow metal tank. The tank was empty.

"Where Elmer performed, no doubt," Allen said.

"Sorry I missed him," Hilks said. "I use the masculine gender only as a courtesy due the name. We humans tend to take sex for granted, even in lower life forms, and we shouldn't."

Bronsky returned and handed Allen an envelope. "I just had these printed up," he said. "I think I'll make a nice profit selling them after the act."

"If I were you," Allen said, "I'd go slow about stocking up."

"Aw—Elmer wouldn't hurt nobody. I've had him almost three years, an' if he'd wanted to eat somebody he'da started on me, wouldn't he? Anyway, he won't even eat meat unless it's ground up pretty fine, an' he don't care much for it then. He's mostly a vegetarian."

Allen took out the glossy prints and passed the top one to Hilks.

"Looks a little like a giant conch shell," Hilks said. "It's much larger, of course. What did it weigh?"

"Three fifty," Bronsky said.

"I would have thought more than that. Has it grown any since you got him?"

Bronsky shook his head. "I figure he's full grown."

"He came from Venus?"

Bronsky nodded.

"I don't recall any customs listing of a creature like this."

Allen was studying the second print. It resembled—vaguely —the painting on the poster. The shell was there, as in the first photo, and protruding out of it was the caricature of a shapely Venus. The outline was hazy but recognizable.

The other photos showed other caricatures—an old bearded man with a pipe, an elephant's head, an entwining winged snake, a miniature rocket ship—all rising out of the cavernous opening.

"How do you do it?" Hilks asked.

"I don't do it," Bronsky said. "Elmer does it."

"Do you mean to say your act is genuine? That the snail actually forms these images?"

"Sure. Elmer loves to do it. He's just a big ham. Show him anyone or anything, and the first thing you know he's looking just like that. If you were to walk up to him, he'd think it over for a few seconds and then he'd come out looking pretty much like you. It's kind of like seeing yourself in a blurred mirror. I use that to close my act—I get some guy up on the stage and

Elmer makes a pretty good reproduction of him. The audience loves it."

Hilks tapped the photo of the distorted Venus. "You didn't find a live model for that."

"Oh, no," Bronsky said. "Not for any of my regular acts. I got a young artist fellow to make some animated film strips for me. I project them onto a screen above the stage. The audience can't see it, but Elmer can. He makes a real good reproduction of that one—the snake hair twists around and the hands make clawing motions at the audience. It goes over big."

"I'll bet," Hilks said. "What does Elmer use for eyes?"

"I don't know. I've wondered about that myself. I've never been able to find any, but he sees better than I do."

"Is it a water creature or a land creature?"

"It doesn't seem to make much difference to him," Bronsky said. "I didn't keep him in water because it'd be hard to tote a big tank of water around. He drank a lot, though."

Hilks nodded and called the commissioner over. "Here's how I see it. Superficially, Elmer resembles some of the terrestrial univalve marine shells. That's undoubtedly deceptive. Life developed along different lines on Venus, and up until now we've found no similarity whatsoever between Terran and Venusian species. That doesn't mean that accidental similarities can't exist. Some of the Terran carnivores produce an acid that etches holes in the shells of the species they prey on. Then there's the common starfish, which paralyzes its victim with acid and then extrudes its stomach outside its body, wraps it around the victim, and digests it. Something like that must have happened to the kids. An acid is the only explanation for the effect of cauterization, and the way their bodies were—absorbed, the doctor said, a very good word—means that the digestive agent has a terrifying corrosive potency. The only puzzling thing about it is how this creature could move fast enough to get clear of the tent and all the way over to that house and surprise three agile children. Frankly, I don't understand how it was able to move at all, but it happened, and it isn't a pleasant thing to think about."

"How did Elmer get away?" Allen asked Bronsky.

"I don't know. We'd just finished a show, and I closed the

curtains and saw the people out of the tent, and then I went back to the stage and he was gone. I didn't know he could move around. He never tried before."

"No one saw him after that?" Allen asked the commissioner.

The commissioner shook his head.

"May I see Elmer's license?" Allen asked Bronsky.

Bronsky stared at him. "Elmer don't need no license!"

Allen said wearily, "Section seven, paragraph nine of the Terran Customs Code, now ratified by all world governments. Any extra-terrestrial life form brought to this planet must be examined by Terran Customs, certified harmless, and licensed. Terran Customs may, at its discretion, place any restrictions it deems necessary upon the custody or use of such life. Did Elmer pass Terran Customs?"

Bronsky brightened. "Oh. Sure. This guy I bought Elmer from, he said all that stuff was taken care of and I wouldn't have any trouble."

"Who was he?"

"Fellow named Smith. I ran into him in a bar in San Diego. Told him I was in show business, and he said he had the best show on Earth in his warehouse. He offered to show it to me, and I walked into this room where there wasn't nothing but a big shell, and the next thing I knew I was looking at myself. I knew it was a natural. He wanted twenty-five grand, which was all the money I had, and I wrote him a check right on the spot. The very next day Elmer and I were in business, and we did well right from the start. As soon as I got enough money together to have the film strips made we did even better. I got a receipt from this guy Smith, and he certified that the twenty-five grand included all customs fees. It's in a deposit box in Phoenix."

"Did Smith give you a Terran Customs license for Elmer?"

Bronsky shook his head.

Allen turned away. "Place this man under arrest, Commissioner."

Bronsky yelped. "Hey—I haven't done anything! Neither has Elmer. You find him and bring him back to me. That's your job."

"My job is to protect the human race from fools like you."

"I haven't done anything!"

"Look," Allen said. "Ten, twelve years ago there was a serious famine in Eastern Asia. It took all the food reserves of the rest of the world to keep the populations from starving. There was no harvest of cereal crops for two years, and it all happened because a young space cadet brought home a Venusian flower for his girl. It was only a potted plant—nothing worth bothering customs about, he thought. But on that plant were lice, Venusian lice. Not many Venusian insects would thrive in Earth's atmosphere, but these did, and they had the food supplies of Japan and China ruined before we knew they were around. By the time we stopped them they were working into India and up into the Democratic Soviet. We spent a hundred million dollars, and finally we had to import a parasite from Venus to help us. That parasite could eventually do as much harm as the lice. It'll be decades before the whole mess is cleaned up.

"We have dozens of incidents like this every year, and each one is potentially disastrous. Even if Elmer didn't kill those kids, he could be carrying bacteria capable of decimating the human race. This is something for you to think about in the years to come. The minimum prison term for having unlicensed alien life in your possession is ten years. The maximum is life."

Bronsky, stricken silent, was led away by Sergeant Darrow.

"Do you suppose there really was a Smith?" the commissioner asked.

"It's likely. There've been a lot of Smiths lately. It was a mistake for the government to dump those surplus spaceships on the open market. A lot of retired spacers picked them up expecting to make a fortune freighting ore. They couldn't make expenses, so some of them took to smuggling in anything they could pick up, figuring that there'd be a nice profit in souvenirs from outer space. Unfortunately, they were right. Who's this?"

A dignified, scholarly looking man entered the tent and stood waiting by the entrance.

"Did you want something?" the commissioner asked.

"I'm Professor Dubois," the man said. "You probably don't remember me, but a short time ago you were asking if anyone had seen that perfidious snail. I haven't seen it, but I can tell you one of the places it went. It broke open one of my display cases and ate an exhibit."

"Ah!" Allen exclaimed. "You'll be from the Exotic Wonders of the Universe. You say the snail ate one of the 'Wonders'?"

"I don't know what else would have wanted it that badly."

"What was it?"

"Venusian moss."

"Interesting. The snail's been on Earth nearly three years, and it probably missed its natural diet. Let's have a look."

A plastic display case at the rear of the tent had been ripped open. Inside lay a bare slab of mottled green rock—Venusian rock.

"When did it happen?" Allen asked.

"I couldn't say. Obviously at a time when the tent was empty."

"None of your customers noticed that a Wonder was missing?"

He shook his head. "They'd think the rock was the exhibit. It's about as interesting as the moss. There wasn't much to it but the color scheme—yellows and reds and blacks with a kind of a sheen."

"And so friend Elmer likes moss. That's an interesting point, since Bronsky claims the snail was by preference a vegetarian. Thank you for letting us know. If you don't mind, we'll take charge of this display case. We might be able to let you have it back later."

"It's ruined anyway. You're welcome to it."

"Would you look after it, Commissioner? Just see that no one touches it until our equipment arrives. I want a close look at some of these Wonders."

The commissioner sighed. "If you say so. But I can't help thinking you two aren't acting overly concerned about this thing. You've been here the best part of two hours, and all you've done is walk around and look at things and ask questions. I've got three hundred men out there in the fields, and what we're mostly worried about is how we're supposed to handle this snail if we happen to catch him."

"Sorry," Allen said. "I should have told you. I have five divisions of army troops being flown in. They're on their way. The corps commander will place this entire county under martial law as soon as he touches down. Another five divisions are under stand-by orders for use when and if the general thinks he needs them. We have a complete scientific laboratory ordered, we've drafted the best scientists we can lay our hands on, and we're reserving one of the Venus frequencies for our own use in case we need information from the scientific stations there. Alien life is unpredictable, and we've had some bitter experiences with it. And—yes, you might say we're concerned about this."

From somewhere in the darkness came the snap of a rifle, and then another, and finally a rattling hum as the weapon was switched to full automatic.

"I didn't expect that," Allen said.

"Why not?" Hilks asked.

"These are regular troops. They shouldn't be shooting at shadows."

"Maybe word got around about what happened to the kids."

"Maybe." Allen went to the door of their tent. Corps Headquarters was a blaze of light; the remainder of the encampment was dark, but the men were stirring nervously and asking one another about the shooting. The full moon lay low on the horizon, silhouetting the orderly rows of tents.

"What were you muttering about just now?" Allen asked.

"I'm still trying to figure out how Elmer got his six-foot shell from one tent to another, and smashed that display, and ate the moss, and got himself across fifty yards of open ground and over a fence into that yard and grabbed off the kids before they saw him coming, and then got clean away. It's enough to make a man mutter."

"It was a much better trick than that," Allen said. "He also did it without leaving any marks. You'd think an object that large and heavy would crush a blade of grass now and then, but Elmer didn't. Which really leaves only one explanation."

"The damned thing can fly."

"Right," Allen said.

"How?"

"It's the world's greatest mimic. Bronsky says so. When it feels like it, it can make like a bird."

Hilks rejected the suggestion profanely. "It must be jet-propelled," he said. "Our own squids can do it in water. It's theoretically possible to do it in air, but in order to lift that much weight, it'd have to pump—let's see, cubic capacity, air pressure—what are you doing?"

"Going back to bed. I'd like to get some sleep, but between the army's shooting and your snoring—did you send a message to Venus?"

"Yes," Hilks said. "I asked for Elmer's pedigree."

"I'll give you two-to-one Venus has never heard of him."

Hilks reflected. "I think fifty-to-one would be fairer odds."

Allen closed his eyes. Hilks continued to mutter. He would not be able to sleep until he had reduced the jet-propelled Elmer to a satisfactory mathematical basis. Allen considered it a waste of time. He had no faith in Earth mathematics when applied to alien life forms.

Hilks turned on a light. A moment later his portable computer hummed to life. Allen turned over and kicked his blanket aside. The night was distressingly warm.

Footsteps crunched outside their tent. A tense voice snapped, "Allen? Hilks?"

"Come in," Allen said. Hilks continued to mutter and to punch buttons on the computer.

The tent flap zipped open, and a very young major stood blinking in at them. "General Fontaine would like to see you."

"Do we have time to dress, or is the general in a hurry?"

"I'd say he's in a powerful hurry."

Allen pulled on his dressing gown and slipped on a pair of shoes. Hilks was out of the tent ahead of him, shuffling along in his pajamas. The camp seemed suddenly wide awake, with voices coming from every tent.

They found General Fontaine in his operations headquarters pacing up and down in front of a map board. An overlay of colored scribbles identified troop positions. The general had aged several years since that afternoon. Obviously he had not been to bed, and he wore the weary, frustrated look of a man who has just realized that he might not get to bed.

"I've lost a man," he announced to Allen.

"How?" Allen asked.

"He's disappeared."

"Without a trace?"

"Not exactly," the general said. "He left his shoes."

Despite strict orders that sentries were to stand duty in pairs, the missing man, Private George Agazzi, had been posted alone on the edge of a small wood. Nearby sentries heard him shout a challenge and then open fire. They could not leave their posts to investigate, but Agazzi's sergeant was on the spot within minutes.

A patrol searched the wood and found no trace of the missing man. Reinforcements were called out, and the search was expanded. Half an hour later a staff officer found Agazzi's rifle, sundry items of equipment, and his shoes in tall grass less than six feet from his post. None of the searchers had seen them.

"Want to have a look?" the general asked.

Hilks shook his head. "In the morning, perhaps. We've already seen something similar, and I doubt that there's anything to be learned there tonight. Perhaps you'd better put three men on a post."

"You think this snail got Agazzi?"

"I'm sure of it."

"He wasn't the best-disciplined soldier in my corps, but he was tough, and he knew how to handle himself. He fired a full clip of atomic pellets, and that would make mincemeat out of any snail. It doesn't make sense. I'd be inclined to think he's gone A.W.O.L. if it weren't for one thing."

"Right," Hilks said. "He wouldn't have left his shoes."

They returned to their tent, and Allen lay awake with the camp stirring around him and sifted through the few facts he had collected. He could not fit them together. He examined each one carefully, testing it, pushing it aside, trying it again. Either he desperately needed more facts, or—could it be that he already had too many?

Patrols passed their tent, and occasionally the soldiers' muttered remarks were sharp enough to be understood. "How often does this thing get hungry?" one wanted to know. Allen wished he knew the answer. He lay awake until dawn.

Allen had worn his facts threadbare, and he could think of only one avenue of exploration still open to him. He had to interview young Johnnie Larkins, who had, through chance or agility, lost only his legs to the thing from Venus. Allen fervently hoped he had lived to tell about it.

General Fontaine established a "Contaminated Zone" centering about the town of Gwinn Center. The first problem, as he saw it, was to contain the thing within this zone. The second problem was to find it and destroy it.

He ringed the zone with armed men and attempted to move all civilians out. Some of the carnival people and a few other crotchety individuals refused to go, one of them being Dr. Anderson. Allen advised against the use of force, so the general contented himself with gloomily forecasting their probable fate and allowed them to remain.

Allen found Dr. Anderson in his home, which was also his office. The front room was a waiting room furnished with comfortable, antique-looking chairs. On the door to the inner office a small sign read, "Doctor is in. Please be seated." Allen ignored it and knocked firmly on the door.

Dr. Anderson emerged with a scowl of stern disapproval on his wrinkled face. "Oh," he said. "It's you. What d'ya want?"

Allen told him. The doctor's scowl deepened, and he said, "Office hours. I couldn't leave before noon, and I'd have to be back by two."

"I rather doubt that you'll be having any patients this morning, Doctor. Gwinn Center's population has been reduced to something like two dozen and all of them are staying home."

"Matter of principle," the doctor said.

"If this mess isn't cleared up, you may never have any patients. I'm hoping that the boy can help us."

Dr. Anderson stroked one withered cheek and continued to scowl. Finally, with an abrupt motion, he turned to the sign on the door and reversed it. "Doctor is out," it read.

"I'll get my hat," he said.

They walked out to the street together, and Allen handed the doctor into his plane. He turned for a last look about the abandoned town and felt a twinge of alarm as somewhere far down the street a door slammed. "There should be troops stationed in town," he told himself. "I'll speak to the general about it."

They flew south. The doctor continued to grumble until Allen patiently explained a second time that the boy would undoubtedly feel more comfortable answering questions with a familiar face present, and then he sulkily settled down to watch the scenery.

Langsford was a modern city, with tall apartment buildings rising from its park-like residential sections. The hospital was part of a vast service complex at the center of the city, a low, web-like structure with narrow, sprawling wings. All of the inner rooms opened into plastic-domed parks.

They found the boy outside his room laughing gaily, a squirrel perched on each arm of his powered chair and a flock of brightly colored birds fluttering about him. The birds flew into a nearby tree when they approached. The squirrels remained motionless.

"Hello, Johnnie," Dr. Anderson said.

The boy smiled at the doctor and then turned large, brown, extremely serious eyes on Allen.

"Found yourself a couple of pets, I see," the doctor said.

"They're my friends," Johnnie said and ceremoniously offered each squirrel a nut.

"Mr. Allen wants to ask you some questions about your accident. Do you feel like talking about it?"

"I don't know much about it," the boy said.

"Can you tell me what happened?" Allen asked.

The boy shook his head. "We were playing. Sharon and Ruthie and me. Then it grabbed me. I couldn't get away. It hurt."

"What did it look like?"

"A rug," the boy said.

Allen pondered that. "What sort of rug?"

"A real pretty rug. It was sailing through the air, and it landed on us."

"What color was it?"

The boy hesitated. "Lots of colors."

Allen scratched his head and tried to envision a sailing, multicolored rug. "A big rug?" he asked.

"Real big."

"As big as a blanket?"

The boy frowned. "Not a real big blanket, I guess."

Dr. Anderson spoke in a low voice. "You can pinpoint the size by the area it covered."

Allen didn't agree, but he smiled and continued his questions. "How high did it fly, Johnnie?"

"Don't know," the boy said.

"Was it attached to something?"

The boy looked puzzled.

"I mean, was it fastened onto something?"

"Don't know."

"Okay, Johnnie. We want to try and catch that rug before it hurts someone else. You've been a help. If you should remember anything else about it, you tell your doctor, and he'll see that I'm told."

They walked away and left the boy with the motionless squirrels.

"Dratted waste of time," Dr. Anderson said.

"Perhaps. There's the matter of colors to consider. Could Elmer make himself different colors? The photos I saw were black and white."

"He could," the doctor said.

"You're sure about that?"

"I was one of the people he did an imitation of. This fellow Bronsky called me up on that platform. I only went out of curiosity. Then that dratted snail did an imitation of me. Made me feel like a dratted fool. But I was wearing a black suit and a red necktie, and it didn't have any trouble with those colors. Showed me wearing a black suit and a red necktie."

"Then that part is all right. As for the part about flying

through the air—I wonder if it can come out of its shell and fly around. That would—perhaps—explain things."

"Don't see what there is to be explained," the doctor grumbled. "Catch the thing and do away with it before it eats someone else. Explain about it afterward if you think you have to."

The doctor had nothing more to say, not even when Allen landed him back in Gwinn Center. He shrugged off Allen's thanks and marched resolutely through his front door. Through the window Allen saw him reverse the sign to read, "Doctor is in. Please be seated." He disappeared into his inner office and closed the door firmly.

When Allen got back to base camp he found that the laboratory plane had arrived, a gigantic old converted transport. The scientists Hilks had requisitioned had also begun to report, but many of them would have little to do until someone brought in Elmer, dead or alive, for them to work on.

Hilks had set up an office for himself in what had been the navigation room, and he looked thoroughly at home as he waved a cigar with one hand and a piece of paper with the other.

"The trouble is," Hilks announced to Allen, "all the experts we need are on Venus, because if they stayed here they'd have so little Venusian life to study that they wouldn't be experts. And if we were to ask them to dash back here to help us cope with one so-called snail, they'd laugh us right out of the Solar System. Did you get anything?"

"Maybe," Allen said. He transferred a pile of books from a chair to the table and seated himself. "Elmer is more talented than we'd thought. He decks himself out in technicolor. The doctor saw him on display and verifies that. And the injured boy says Elmer looked like a pretty rug flying through the air."

"We figured he had to fly," Hilks said.

"Yeah. But that youngster is no dunce, and if he saw a big shell come whizzing through the air, I don't think he'd call it a rug."

"What do you want us to do?"

"We've got to come up with something that'll help Fontaine capture it and keep it captured."

"Uh huh," Hilks said, scowling. "I've been studying the report on Private Agazzi. He did empty a full clip at whatever it was he saw, and his officer thinks he was a good enough shot to hit what he aimed at. Add the fact that while you were gone a patrol spotted Elmer skimming across a field. They called it skimming. He vanished into a large grove of trees, and I do mean vanished. The general had a regiment standing by for just that contingency, and he dropped them around the grove in nothing flat. That was two hours ago, and they still haven't found anything."

"Are any of them missing?"

Hilks shook his head. "Maybe Elmer hasn't had time to get hungry again. We've come up with a thought that's somewhat less than pleasant. Elmer might be able to reproduce all by himself, and if he likes Earth enough to start populating the planet with baby snails, this continent could become a rather unpleasant place to live."

"Have you come up with anything at all?"

"Sure. One of the boys has designed a nifty steel net to be dropped out of a plane—if Elmer is ever spotted from a plane. We're also working on some traps, but it's a little hard to decide what to use for bait, since the only thing Elmer seems to like to eat is people. We might ask for volunteers and put cages inside the traps. Touchy proposition, we don't know what sort of a cage would keep Elmer out, just as we also don't know what sort of trap would keep him in."

"Did you do anything with that plastic display case Elmer broke into?" Allen asked.

"No," Hilks said. "I had it brought over here, but I completely forgot about it. Let's go look at it now. Meyers, find someone who knows something about Venusian moss and fungus and related subjects. Since Elmer likes that particular moss enough to break a display case to get it, maybe we could use it for bait."

"Never mind," Allen said. "We're slipping on this thing, Hilks. That exhibit was licensed, so Terran Customs will have a complete file on it. I'll ask for a report."

Allen copied the license number and called his office from the plane's communications room, using his own emergency channel. Ten minutes later he bounded wildly into Hilks's office.

"What's the matter?" Hilks demanded.

"Everything. Get this Professor Dubois over here and fast. That exhibit was never registered. The license is a forgery."

The professor waved his arms excitedly. "I never dreamed!" he exclaimed. "I have been extremely careful with all of my exhibits. It does not pay not to be careful. But you must admit that the license looks genuine."

"You say you bought the exhibit on the West Coast," Allen said. "Tell us about it."

"Let's see—it was maybe three years ago. I was showing in upstate California. Fellow came in one day and said he was breaking up his own exhibit and had a few things left to sell. He made them sound good, and I went all the way to San Diego to see what he had. It really wasn't bad stuff—it would have been a good basic collection for someone starting out, but there wasn't anything there that would have helped my collection. I took that one because I hated to waste a trip and he made me a good price. And it was a pretty thing."

"Could you describe this man?"

"I doubt it. It's been a long time. His name? Oh—that I remember. It was Smith."

"Describe this 'moss' again, please."

"Well, like I said, it was pretty stuff. Vivid colors, red and black and yellow and white without any special pattern. It had a nice sheen to it—looked like a hunk of thick blanket."

"Or a hunk of rug?" Allen suggested.

"Well, yes. I suppose you could say rug."

Allen backed over to a chair and sat down heavily. "The fact that it was small and thick means nothing. 'Thick' things sometimes unfold into objects many yards square. Hilks, take a look at that case. Take a good look. I want to know if it was smashed by something breaking into it, or by something breaking out of it."

Hilks bent over the case. "It bulges," he announced. "If the snail could apply suction, it might have made it bulge this way."

Allen went to have a look. "The sides bulge, too," he said. "It looks as though something inside applied force in all directions, and the top gave first."

Hilks nodded slowly. "Yes, it does look that way. Without a demonstration to the contrary by the snail, I'd say that something broke out of here."

Allen returned to his chair. For twenty years he had been studying Venus and all things Venusian, assimilating every scrap of information and every report that came his way. Now he could rearrange his facts, and this time he could make them fit.

"Ever hear of a Venusian Night Cloak?" he asked.

They shook their heads.

"You have now. Tell General Fontaine to call off his snail hunt. This problem may be a lot worse than we'd thought."

They sat around a table in the large upper room of the lab plane—Allen, Hilks, General Fontaine, and Professor Dubois. Hilks's scientists had crowded into the room behind them.

Allen started the projector. The screen erupted a Venusian jungle, its blanched vegetation having a revolting, curdled appearance through the steaming mist. The camera shifted upward, taking in a square of greenish sky. In the distance, just above the seething treetops, appeared a blob of color. It enlarged slowly as it sailed toward them, a multicolored flat surface that rippled and twisted and curled in flight.

"That's it!" the professor exclaimed. "The markings are just like my moss."

It came on until it filled the screen. Suddenly it plummeted away, and the camera followed it until it disappeared into the jungle.

Allen switched off the projector. "Officially that's the closest anyone has gotten to one," he said. "Now we know otherwise. My feeling is that a number of scientists missing and presumed dead in the Great Doleman Swamp got rather too close to a Night Cloak."

The professor looked stricken. "This—my moss—killed those innocent children?"

"None of our facts fit the snail. All of them fit the Night Cloak."

"Why do they call it a Night Cloak?" the general asked.

"It was first observed at night, and it seems most active then. It grows to an enormous size, and as far as anyone on Venus knows—and don't forget there's a lot of the planet to be explored yet—it is found only in the Great Doleman Swamp. That's the reason so little is known about it. A jungle growing in a swamp isn't the easiest place for field work, and a Venusian jungle is impossible. Stations on the edge of the swamp occasionally observe the Night Cloaks, but always from a distance. They seem to be a unique life form, and the scientists were naturally curious about them. Twice expeditions were sent out to capture a specimen, and both parties disappeared without a trace. No one thought to blame the Night Cloaks—there are enough other things in that swamp that can do away with a man, especially some of the giant amphibians.

"This film strip was shot by a lucky pilot who happened to be hanging motionless over the swamp. A Night Cloak won't approach a moving plane. The scientific reports contain little but speculation. Frankly, gentlemen, we already know more about the Night Cloak than Venus does, and we're going to have to learn in a hurry something Venus hasn't discovered in a hundred years of field work: How to catch one."

"This fellow Smith caught one," Professor Dubois said.

"It was obviously a young one, and it's possible that they have periods of dormancy when one could be picked up easily—fortunately for Smith. Something about being transported and placed in Earth's atmosphere kept it dormant. It's our misfortune that it didn't die."

General Fontaine was drumming on the table with his fingers. "You say we know more about them than Venus knows. Just what do we know?"

"We know that you can't shoot one. Private Agazzi probably

punched a lot of holes in it, but how would you aim at vital organs of a creature thirty feet square and who knows what fraction of an inch thick? We know that it has strength. It broke that plastic display case apart. We know a few unpleasant things about its diet and how it ingests food. We even know that its victims are likely to leave their shoes behind, which may or may not be a vital bit of information. And we know that our contaminated zone isn't worth a damn because a Night Cloak can fly right over the ground troops and probably already has."

"I'll have to call up all the planes I can get ahold of," the general said. "I'll have to reorganize the ground troops so I can rush them in when the thing is sighted."

"Excuse me, sir," said the young scientist named Meyers. "What was that you said a moment ago about shoes?"

"Just a little peculiarity of our Night Cloak," Allen told him. "It will totally consume a human body, and it doesn't mind clothing, but shoes absolutely do not appeal to it. It eats the feet and stockings right out of them, sometimes, but it leaves the shoes. I don't know what it means, but it's one positive thing we do know."

"Just a moment," Meyers said. He pushed his way out of the room and ran noisily down the stairway. He returned waving a newspaper. "I picked this up when I came through Langsford this morning," he said.

He passed the paper to Allen, who glanced at the headline and shrugged. "Monster still at large."

"That isn't exactly news to us," General Fontaine said.

"It's down at the bottom of the page," Meyers said. "A woman went for a walk last night and disappeared. They found her handbag in a park on the edge of Langsford, and a short distance away they found her shoes."

The general sucked in his breath sharply and reached for the paper. Hilks leaned back, folded his hands behind his head, and looked at the ceiling.

"Langsford," Allen said slowly. "Forty miles. But it also got Private Agazzi last night."

"If we make this public, it'll start a panic," General Fontaine said. "We'll have to evacuate the eastern half of the state. And if we don't make it public—"

"We'll have to make it public," Allen said.

"I'll have to order in my five reserve divisions. I'll need them for police work, and I'll need their transport to get the people out. God knows how far that thing may have gone by now."

"Message from Venus," a voice called. It was handed to Hilks, who read it and tossed it onto the table disgustedly.

"I asked Venus about the mollusk. They've checked all their records, and as far as they know it has no Venusian relatives. They ask, please, if we will kindly send it along to them when we're finished with it, preferably alive. They'd like to study it."

General Fontaine got to his feet. "Shall I take care of the news release?" he asked Allen.

"I'll handle it," Allen said and reached for a piece of paper. He studied a map for a moment, and then he wrote, "Notice to the populations of Kansas, Oklahoma, Arkansas, Missouri, Iowa, Nebraska, and Colorado."

For five days Allen sat at a desk in the lab plane answering inquiries, sifting through reports and rumors, searching vainly for a fact, an idea, that he could convert into a weapon. The lab's location was changed five times and he hardly noticed the moves.

The list of victims grew with horrifying rapidity. A farmer at work in his fields, a housewife hurrying along a quiet street to visit a friend, a sheriff's deputy investigating a report of looting in an abandoned town, an off-duty soldier who left his bivouac area for reasons best known to himself—Allen compiled the list, and Hilks added the shoes to his collection.

"This may not be the half of it," Allen said worriedly. "With so many people on the move, it'll be weeks before we get reports on everyone that's missing."

General Fontaine's Contaminated Area doubled and tripled and tripled again. On the third day the Night Cloak was sighted near the Missouri-Kansas border, and the populations of four states were in panicky flight.

That same night old Dr. Anderson got a call through to

Allen from Gwinn Center. "That dratted thing is fussing around my window," he said.

"That can't be," Allen told him. "It was sighted two hundred miles from there this afternoon."

"I'm watching it while I talk to you," the doctor said.

"I'll send someone right away."

They found Dr. Anderson's shoes near a broken window, directly under the sign that read, "Doctor is in."

The next morning an air patrol sighted an abandoned ground car just across the Missouri border. It landed to investigate and found mute evidence of high tragedy. A family of nine had been fleeing eastward. The car had broken down, and the driver got out to make repairs. At that moment the horror had struck. In and around the car were nine pairs of shoes.

Hilks was losing weight, and he had also lost much of his good-natured nonchalance. "That thing *can't* travel that fast," he said. "The car must have been sitting there for a couple of days."

"Fontaine has traced it," Allen told him. "The family left home yesterday afternoon, and it'd have reached the place the car was found about ten o'clock last night."

"That's when the doctor called."

"Right," Allen said.

Lieutenant Gus Smallet was one small cog in the enormous observation grid General Fontaine hung over eastern Kansas and western Missouri. His plane was a veteran road-hopper, a civilian model pressed into service when the general received emergency authority to grab anything that would fly. It was armed only with a camera that Smallet had supplied himself.

Smallet flew slowly in a straight line, his plane being one of a vast formation of slow-moving observation planes. It was his third day on this fruitless search, his third day of taking off into the pre-dawn darkness and flying until daylight faded, and he was wondering which he would succumb to first, fatigue or boredom. His head ached. Other portions of his anatomy ached worse, especially that which had been crushed against an uncomfortable, thinly padded seat for more hours than

Smallet cared to remember. His movements had become mechanical, his thoughts had long since taken flight to other, more pleasant subjects than a Venusian Night Cloak, and he had stopped asking himself whether he would recognize the damned thing if he happened to see it.

Suddenly, against the dark green of a cluster of trees, he glimpsed a fleck of color. He slipped into a shallow dive, staring hypnotically as the indistinct blur grew larger and took on shape.

A bellow from his radio jolted Smallet back to reality. His sharp-eyed commanding officer, whose plane was a speck somewhere on the horizon, was telling him to stop horsing around and keep his altitude.

"I see the damned thing!" Smallet shouted. "I see—"

What he did see so startled him that he babbled incoherently and did not realize until afterward that he had instinctively flipped the switch on his camera. It was well that he had done so. His story was received with derision, and his commanding officer sniffed his breath suspiciously and muttered words that sounded direly like *Courts-Martial*.

Then the developed film was brought in, and what Smallet had seen was there for all to gape at.

Not one Night Cloak, but five.

It was dark by the time the transports started pouring ground troops into the area. They lost seven men that night and saw nothing at all.

Solly Hertz was an ordnance sergeant with ability and imagination. So when Hertz told his captain that he wanted to go to division headquarters to discuss an idea he had about these Night Cloak things, the captain paled at the thought of losing the one man who could keep his electronic equipment operating. He confined Hertz to the company area and mopped his brow over the narrow margin of his escape.

Hertz went A.W.O.L., by-passed division and corps and army, and invaded the sanctuary of the supreme air commander. That much-harassed general encountered Hertz through the accident of seeing a squad of military police leading him away. Fortunately he had enough residual curiosity to inquire about the offense and ask Hertz what he wanted.

"One of your guys sees one of these Night Cloaks," Hertz said. "What's he supposed to do about it?"

"Blast it," the general said promptly.

"Won't do any good," Hertz said. "Slugs and shrapnel just punch holes in it, and that don't bother it none. And a contact fuse wouldn't even go off when it hit. It's like shooting at tissue paper."

"You think you can do something about that?" the general asked.

"I got an atomic mini-rocket with a proximity fuse. It'll trigger just before it hits the thing. It'll *really* blast it."

"You're sure it won't go off at the wrong time and cost me a pilot?"

"Not the way I got it fixed."

"How many have you got?"

"One," Hertz said. "How many do you want?"

"Just for a starter, about five thousand. Tell me what you need and get to work on it."

Captain Joe Carr took off the next morning equipped with two of Hertz's rockets. Before he entered his plane he crossed fingers on both hands and spat over his left shoulder. And once inside the plane he went through a brisk ceremony of clicking certain switches on and off with certain predetermined fingers. Having thus dutifully sacrificed to the goddess of luck, he was not at all surprised an hour later when he sighted a Night Cloak.

It was a big one. It was enormous, and Carr glowed with satisfaction as he made a perfect approach, fired one rocket, and circled to see if another was needed.

It was not. The enormous, rippling surface was suddenly seared into nothingness—almost. The rocket hit it dead center, and when Carr completed his turn he saw the Night Cloak looking, as he said later, like the rind off a piece of bologna.

But even as he yelped news of his triumph into the radio, the rind collapsed crazily and parted, and four small, misshapen Night Cloaks flew gently downward to disappear into the trees.

Private Edward Walker was thinking about shoes. Night Cloaks never ate shoes. Flesh and bones and clothing and maybe even metal, but not shoes. That was official.

"All right," Walker told himself grimly. "If one of those things comes around here, I'll kick the life out of it."

He delivered a vicious practice kick and felt very little the better for it; and the truth was that Private Edward Walker had excellent reason for his uneasiness.

His regiment was deployed around a small grove of trees. Two Night Cloaks had been sighted entering the trees. The place had been kept under observation, and as far as anyone knew they were still there, but the planes hovering overhead, and the cautious patrols of lift-equipped soldiers that looped skittishly over the grove, from one side to the other, had caught no further glimpse of them.

Walker had put in an hour of lift-patrolling himself, and he hadn't liked it. He had the uncomfortable feeling, as he floated over the trees and squinted down into the shadows, that someone was using him for bait. This was maybe excusable if it promised to accomplish anything, but so far as anyone knew these Cloaks had the pernicious habit of taking the bait and never getting caught. The casualty list was growing with appalling speed, the Cloaks were getting fat—or at least getting bigger—and not one of them had been destroyed.

But the brass hats had tired of that nonsense and decided to make a stand. This insignificant grove of trees could well be the Armageddon of the human race.

Walker's captain had been precise about it. "If these things go on multiplying, it means the end of humanity. We've got to stop them, and this is the place and we're the guys to do it."

The men looked at each other, and a sergeant was bold enough to ask a question. "Just how are we going to knock them off?"

"They're working that out right now," the captain said. "I'll let you know as soon as I get the Word."

That had been early morning. Now it was noon, and they were still waiting for the Word. Private Walker felt more like bait with each passing minute. He looked again at his indestructible shoe leather. "I'll kick the life out of them," he muttered.

"Walker!" his sergeant bellowed. "You going off your nut? Sit down and relax."

Walker walked toward the sergeant. "It's true, isn't it? That business about the Cloaks not eating shoes?"

Sergeant Altman took a cautious glance at his own shoes and nodded.

"Shoes are made out of leather," Walker said. "Why don't we make us some suits out of leather? And gloves, too?"

The sergeant scratched his head fretfully. "Let's talk to the captain."

They talked to the captain. The captain rushed the two of them off to see a colonel, and in no time at all they were in the hallowed presence of a general, a big, intense man whose glance chilled Walker to the soles of his feet and who paced irritably back and forth while Walker stammered his fanciful question about leather suits and gloves.

When he finished, the general stopped pacing. "Congratulations, Private Walker," he said. "Someone should have thought of this three weeks ago, but no one did. It's men like you who make our army great. I'll see that you get a medal for this, and I'll also see that you get all the leather you want."

They saluted and turned away, both of them stunned at the realization that they'd been granted the honor of testing Walker's idea. It didn't help when they heard the general say, just before they passed out of hearing, "Darned silly notion. Do you think it'd work?"

Dusk was dropping down on them when the "leather" arrived. Walker slipped on a leather jacket and boots that reached his knees. He wrapped pieces of leather around his upper legs and tied them on with strips of leather. He fashioned a rough leather skirt for himself, ignoring the snickers of those watching. Five others did the same—three privates, the sergeant and the captain. The captain tossed leather hats to them, and gloves, and Walker carefully worked the sleeves of his jacket down into the gloves.

"All right," the captain said. "This will have to do. If it works they'll design a one-piece leather suit with something to protect the face, but we'll have to show them that it works. Let's get in there before it's too dark to see."

The grove was already ringed with lights that laced the half-darkness with freakish shadows as far as they were able to penetrate. The captain arranged them in a tight formation, himself in the lead and the sergeant bringing up the rear. A quick glance to see that all was ready, a nod, and they worked their way forward.

After an advance of ten yards the captain held up his hand. They stopped, and Walker, in his position on the right flank, looked about uneasily—up, down, sideways. A light breeze stirred the treetops high overhead. From the sky came the hollow buzz of a multitude of planes. The noise had a remote, unreal quality.

The captain signaled, and they moved on. Someone stumbled and swore, and the captain hissed, "Silence!"

They reached the far side of the grove and turned back. The tension had lifted somewhat; they spread out and began to walk faster. Walker suddenly realized that he was perspiring under the leather garments, that his inner clothing was sopped with sweat.

"I could do with a bath," he muttered, and the captain silenced him with a wave of his hand.

At the center of the grove they wheeled off at an angle. Walker became momentarily separated from the others when he detoured around a dense clump of bushes. There was a warning shout, and as he whirled the Night Cloak was upon him.

He shielded his face with one arm and swung a clenched fist. His hand punched a gaping hole, and he withdrew it and swung again. There was almost no resistance to his blows, and he riddled the pulsating, multicolored substance that draped over him. He had a momentary feeling of exultation. The leather worked. It was protecting him, and he would fix this Cloak but good. He punched and clawed and tore, and huge pieces came away in his grasp. Someone was beside him trying to tear the Cloak away, and he had a glimpse of a furious battle with the other Night Cloak taking place a short distance away.

Then he was completely enveloped, and he screamed with agony as a searing, excruciating pain encircled one knee and then the other. There were several hands fumbling about him, now, pulling shreds of Night Cloak from his struggling body. He raised both arms to protect his face and became aware for the first time of a vile odor. Then the thing flowed, slithered around his arms and found his face, and he lost consciousness.

He awoke gazing at the restful pale gray ceiling of a hospital.

Someone in the next bed chuckled. "Came around, did you? It's about time."

He turned. Sergeant Altman sat on the edge of the bed grinning broadly. Both of his wrists were bandaged; otherwise he seemed unhurt. "How do you feel?" he asked.

Walker felt the bandage that covered most of his face. "It hurts like the devil," he said.

"Sure. You got a good stiff dose of it, too--around your knees and on your face. But the doc says you'll be as good as new after some skin grafts, and you're a lot better off than Lyle. It didn't get your eyes."

"What happened?" Walker asked.

"Well, the leather works good. None of us got hurt except where we weren't protected or where the Cloaks could get underneath the leather. So now they'll be making those one-piece leather suits with maybe a thick plastic to protect the face. All of us are heroes, especially you."

"What happened to the Cloaks?"

"Oh, we tore them into about a hundred pieces each."

Walker nodded his satisfaction.

"And then," Altman went on, "the pieces flew away."

Hilks had a scientific headquarters set up near what had been a sleepy little town north of Memphis. It was a deserted town, now, in a deserted countryside where no living thing moved, and the bustling activity around the lab plane seemed strangely inappropriate, like a frolic at a funeral.

John Allen dropped his plane neatly into a vacant spot among the two dozen planes that were parked nearby. He stood looking at the lab plane for a moment before he walked toward it, and when he did move it was with the uncertain step of an outsider who expects at any moment to be ordered away.

At this moment the Night Cloaks were, as a general had put it that very morning, none of his business.

Two weeks previously his assignment had been cancelled and his authority transferred to the military high command. It was not to be considered a demotion or a reprimand, his superiors told him. On the contrary, he would receive a citation for his work. His competence, and his years of devotion to duty, had enabled him to quickly recognize the menace for what it was and take the best possible action. He had identified the Night Cloak on the sketchiest of evidence, and no one could suggest anything that he should have done but didn't.

But control of the investigation was passed to the military because the Night Cloaks had assumed the dimensions of a national catastrophe that threatened to become international. The nation's top military men could not be placed under the orders of a civilian employee of an extra-national organization.

"Can I continue the investigation on my own?" Allen demanded.

"Take a vacation," his chief said with a smile. "You've earned it."

So Allen had taken vacation leave and immediately returned to the zone of action. Unfortunately, he was temperamentally unsuited to the role of observer. He made suggestions, he criticized, and he attempted to prod the authorities into various kinds of action, and that morning a general had ordered him out of the Contaminated Zone and threatened to have him shot if he returned.

The lab plane was inside the Contaminated Zone, but word of Allen's banishment seemed not to have reached it. A few scientists recognized him and greeted him warmly. He went directly to Hilks's office, and there he found Hilks sitting moodily at his desk and gazing fixedly at a bottle that stood in front of him.

Allen exclaimed, "Where did you get it?"

In the bottle lay a jagged fragment, splotched red and yellow and black, that twisted and curled and uncurled.

"Didn't you hear about the great leather battle?" Hilks asked.

"I heard," Allen said.

"Great fight while it lasted. One small infantry patrol managed to convert two Cloaks into about a hundred cloaks, and this thing—" He nodded at the bottle. "This thing got left behind. It was only an inch long and a quarter of an inch wide, and it was too small to fly. I think one of the men must have stepped on the edge of a Cloak and pinched it off. Anyway, it was found afterward, so we've been studying it. I started feeding it insects, and then I gave it a baby mouse, and the thing literally grows while you watch it. Now it's grown big enough to fly, so I've stopped feeding it."

"But this is just what you needed!" Allen exclaimed. "Now you can find a way to wipe the things out!"

"Yeah? How? We've tried every poison we could think of, not to mention a nitric acid solution that Ferguson dreamed up. It seems to like the stuff. We've tried poison gases, including some hush-hush things the military flew in. You can see how healthy it looks. Now I have my entire staff trying to think up experiments, and I'm just sitting here hating the thing."

"Anything new from Venus?"

"Yeah. They found a cousin of Elmer the snail, so they kindly let us know that we could keep ours. Good joke, eh? I sent them my congratulations and told them the Night Cloaks have already eaten Elmer. Since the Cloaks absorb bones, they probably can absorb snail shells, too. Elmer's kind may be one of their favorite foods."

"What does Venus have to say about the Night Cloaks?"

"Well, they're very interested in what we've been able to tell them, and they thank us for the information. They're going to keep their research teams out of the Great Doleman Swamp until we can tell them how to cope with the things. Other than that, nothing."

"Too bad. I'd hoped they might know something."

"It's a lot worse than you realize. Venus has been so damned smug about the whole catastrophe that some of our politicians have decided to resent that. There's a movement afoot to ban travel to Venus and close down all the Venusian scientific stations. The other planets may be next, and then perhaps even the moon. After triumphantly moving out across the Solar System and hopefully taking aim at the stars, man crawls ignominiously back into his shell. Some of the pessimists think it may take us generations to handle the Cloaks, and in the meantime the Mississippi basin will become uninhabitable as far north as Minnesota and perhaps above the Canadian border in summer. Whatever happens, I'm betting that the well-dressed man will be wearing a lot of leather. The well-dressed woman, too. Do you have any bright ideas for us to work on?"

"I ran out of bright ideas on the third day," Allen said.

"If your mind isn't occupied with anything else, you might work on this one: Where are all the Night Cloaks?"

"The military seems to be keeping good track of them. That's one thing it does well."

"We have a rough tabulation of the minimum number that should be around, and we have records of all of the sightings. As far as we can tell, about ninety per cent have disappeared."

"We figured they had periods of dormancy."

"Sure. But if they're going dormant on us, why hasn't someone found a dormant Night Cloak somewhere? We're worried because we have no notion of what their range is. If they ever get established in the Central and South American jungles, it *will* take us generations to root them out."

"Do you mind if I hang around?" Allen asked. "The last friend I had on the general staff just ordered me out of the Contaminated Zone, but I don't think he'll come here looking for me."

Hilks grinned. "What have you been up to?"

"I keep giving advice even when I'm not supposed to. I raised a ruckus because I didn't see much sense in picking Night Cloaks apart just to make more and smaller Night Cloaks. And then they were designing a new leather uniform to be used in Cloak hunting, and I suggested that instead of wearing such ghastly uncomfortable armor they just give everyone a bath in tannic acid, or whatever the stuff is they use to make leather, and soak their clothing in it at the same time. That was when he threw me out. He said he had ten million scientists telling him what to do, and he had to put up with them, but he didn't have to put up with me. So—what's the matter?"

"Tannic acid?" Hilks said.

"Isn't that the stuff? Probably it'd dry up or evaporate or something and not work anyway, but I thought—"

Hilks was already on his way to the door. "Meyers!" he shouted. "Get your crew in here. We have work to do."

By coincidence Allen entered the room first. The general, looking up sharply from his desk, flushed an unhealthy crimson and leaped to his feet. "You! I told you—"

Hilks stepped around Allen. "Meet my assistant," he said. "Name of Allen."

The general sat down again. "All right. I have my orders. Hilks and three assistants. I have the protective clothing ready for you, and I have a place picked out for you and a patrol to take you there."

"Good," Hilks said. "Let's get going."

"My orders also say that I'm to satisfy myself as to the soundness of whatever it is you propose to do."

"We've developed a spray we'd like to try out on the Cloaks," Hilks said.

"What'll it do to them?"

"You know we have a specimen to work on? The spray seems to anesthetize it. Of course there's a difference between spraying a Cloak sliver in a bottle and spraying a full-sized Cloak in open air."

"You really don't know, then."

"Of course not. That's why we're making the experiment."

"You're asking me to risk the lives of my men—"

"Nope. All we want them to do is show us where the Night Cloaks are and get out of the way. I'm not even risking the lives of my own men. Allen and I will do the testing."

The general stood up. "Tell me. I'm not asking for a prediction, damn it. Do you think this stuff might work?"

"We've had a lot of disappointments, General," Hilks said. "We're fresh out of predictions. But yes, we think it just might work."

"And if it doesn't?"

"The scientific staff will have a couple of openings. That's not much of a risk for a general to take, is it?"

The general grinned. "You're brave men. Anything you want, take it. And—good luck!"

As Allen dropped the plane into the small clearing, the pine forest took on an unexpectedly gloomy aspect. "Cover us while we're dressing," Allen said. He and Hilks climbed out and quickly slipped into the leather suits.

Meyers and another young scientist named Wilcox watched them anxiously. "Wasn't there a better place than this?" Meyers asked.

Allen shook his head. "All the other locations are swampy. Night Cloaks seem to be attracted to swamps, but I'm not. Also, they only saw two of them in this area. Two are enough for beginners like Hilks and me."

"Sure you don't want us to come along?" Meyers asked, as they donned their spray tanks.

Hilks shook his head. "One of the problems has been the total absence of witnesses. If we'd known exactly what happened with each victim, maybe we'd have solved this long ago. You're our witnesses. You're to record everything we say, and we'll try to describe it so you can understand what's happening. If we don't come back, you'll know what went wrong."

Meyers nodded unhappily. They fastened their plastic face guards, picked up the spray guns, and waved a cheerful farewell.

"No undergrowth," Allen observed as they entered the trees.

"It's a Co-op Forest," Hilks said.

"That means we're trespassing."

"So are the Night Cloaks."

They walked briskly for a couple of miles, turned, and started to circle back. "Better check in with Meyers," Allen said. "He'll be turning somersaults."

Hilks switched on his radio. "Haven't seen a thing," he announced.

"Man, you must be blind!" Meyers blurted at them. "There was one right overhead when you started out. It followed you."

They turned quickly and stared upward. For a moment they saw only the cloudless sky through the treetops, and then a blur of color flashed past.

"Okay," Hilks said. "It's flying above the trees—waiting for reinforcements, maybe. We'll keep moving toward the plane. When they attack we'll put a couple of nice big trees at our backs so they won't be able to get at us from behind. If I can find a tree as big around as I am, that is."

"Keep your radios on," Meyers said.

"Right."

They moved at a steady pace, keeping close together and taking turns looking upward.

"Two of them, now," Hilks announced. "They're circling. They look like small ones."

Two minutes later it was Allen's turn. "I just counted three," he said. "No, four. They're coming down—*get ready!*"

The Cloaks dropped through the trees with amazing speed. They plummeted, and Allen, backing up to a tree, had no time for more than the split-second observation that they were unusually small, one being no more than a yard across. All four of them curved toward him. He gave the first one the spray at ten feet and then cut it off. The Cloaks were gone.

Hilks was chuckling as he talked with Meyers. "They got one whiff of the stuff and beat it."

"Now we won't know what'll happen to the one I sprayed," Allen said.

Hilks swore. "I didn't think about that. The most we can claim is that they don't particularly like the stuff."

"Don't be too sure," Allen said. "Here they come again."

They were wary. They dipped down slowly, circled, sailed in and out among the trees. Only the small one ventured close, and it shot upward when Allen gave it a blast of spray.

"For what it's worth," Allen said, "the small ones are hungrier than the big ones."

"It figures," Hilks said.

Meyers, sitting far away in the plane, made unintelligible noises.

The Cloaks did not return immediately. Allen and Hilks peered upward searchingly, and finally Allen asked, "What do we do now?"

"Add the score and go home, I suppose. The stuff doesn't have the punch we hoped for, none of them dropped unconscious at our feet, but at the same time we can claim a limited success. It drives them off, which is more than anything else was able to accomplish. We can develop pressurized containers for self-defense and put the chemists to work making the stuff more potent. Shall we go back?"

"Not yet," Allen said. "Here they come again."

They came, and they continued to come. They seemed not to have noticed Hilks in their first rushes, but now they divided their attention and swooped down in pairs again and again. They were coming closer before they turned upward, flying through the clouds of spray. Once the small one brushed against Allen.

"They can't be *that* hungry," Hilks said.

"No. They're angry. That's what the spray does to them. It maddens them. Are you listening, Meyers?"

"We'd better get moving," Hilks said. "The spray won't last forever. Let's leapfrog. I'll cover you, and then you cover me."

Meyers cut in. "If you can find a clearing, I'll pick you up."

"We'll let you know," Hilks said. "In the meantime, keep a close watch on the forest. With them on our backs we might miss your clearing."

"Right," Meyers said.

Allen made a short dash, placed a tree at his back, and turned to cover Hilks. The sudden movement seemed to infuriate the Cloaks. All four shot after Allen. Three of them turned away as he pointed the spray upward. The small Cloak hovered over him for a moment, taking the full, drenching blast. Then the pressure faded, the spray gun sputtered and cut off, and the Cloak fell upon Allen.

Allen thrust at it, but it encircled and clung to his arm. Hilks raced toward him, drenching both Allen and the Cloak with spray. Pain seared and stabbed at Allen's arm, and he staggered backward and fell. He must have blacked out, for he had no memory of the moment when the Cloak released him. He regained consciousness with Hilks standing over him and turning aside the Cloaks with blasts of spray. He pushed himself to a sitting position and stared down at the throbbing numbness that had been his arm.

"Are you all right?" Hilks asked anxiously. "Can you walk?"

"I—think so." Allen got up unsteadily. "My spray is gone."

"I know. You started before I did, but I can't have much left."

Allen was examining his arm.

"Bad?" Hilks asked.

"Clear to the bone in one place," Allen said. "Fortunately it's not bleeding."

"So we've learned another thing," Hilks said. "Even leather won't stop them when they're riled up or really hungry."

"Can we do anything?" Meyers asked.

"Just watch for us. We'll have to make a run for it. We'll start after their next rush. Ready?"

"Ready," Allen said.

They darted off through the trees.

But the Cloaks were after them in a fluttering rush. Hilks turned, warded them off, and they ran again.

"It's no good," Hilks panted. "My spray is almost finished. Not much pressure left. Any ideas?"

Allen did not answer. Hilks sprayed again, turned for another dash, and fell headlong over the protruding edge of a large rock. He scrambled to his feet and both of them stood staring, not at the circling Cloaks, but at the rock, which inexplicably humped up out of the ground and seemed to float away. After a dozen feet it bumped to the ground. Encrusted dirt fell away from it.

"The devil!" Allen breathed. "It's Bronsky's snail. And look at the size of it!"

"Here come the Cloaks," Hilks said. He aimed the spray gun.

But he did not use it. As the Cloaks dropped down through the trees, a tongue-like ribbon of flesh shot out from the enormous shell, broadened, folded back, and dropped to the ground with a convulsive shudder of satisfaction. And the Cloaks were gone.

They watched in fascination as the flesh heaved and twisted and finally subsided and began slowly to withdraw.

Meyers, screaming wildly into the radio, finally aroused them. "Are you all right?" he demanded.

"Sure," Hilks said. "Everything is all right now."

"What about the Cloaks?"

"They've just been eaten."

"What did you say? Beaten?"

"Eaten," Hilks said. "I have the picture now. All of it. How about you?"

Allen nodded. "The snail is the Cloak's natural enemy. Or the Cloak is its favorite food. This one was more or less happy with Bronsky until one day it smelled or otherwise sensed a Night Cloak in the vicinity. If we hadn't put an army to beating the woods and shooting at it, it probably would have eliminated the menace at once. As soon as we stopped bothering it, it started eating Cloaks, and it's been eating them ever since. That's where the missing Cloaks went. They aren't hibernating, or migrating, they're in the snail. Look how it's grown! How big did Bronsky say it was?"

"About six feet."

"It's ten feet now. At least. There's the answer to our Cloak problem. Forget the spray and the leather clothing. Clear everyone out and leave it to Elmer. Have Venus ship us the snail they have and as many more as they can find. Are you recording, Meyers?"

"Recording," Meyers said happily. "I got the whole thing. Just as the Cloaks were about to finish you off, that snail came galloping up and ate them."

"Not exactly," Allen said. "But close enough. What's Elmer doing now?"

"It sees us," Hilks said.

They watched. The pinkish flesh flowed out slowly, thickened, stood upright. Then, before their disbelieving eyes, it suddenly took shape and color and became the snaky caricature of a once-lovely Venus.

"Allen!" Hilks hissed. "That thing has a memory! It has the proportions wrong, but the image is still recognizable."

"It thinks we're an audience," Allen said. "So it's performing. Bronsky said it was just a big ham." He walked toward it.

"Watch yourself!" Hilks said sharply.

Allen ignored him. He approached the snail, stood close to it, looked up at the wreathing head of Venus.

The Venus collapsed abruptly. The flesh quivered, thrust up again, and became a hazy, misshapen caricature of John Allen, complete with face mask, wounded arm, and dangling spray gun. Somewhere behind him he heard Hilks choking with laughter. Allen ignored him. He extended his sound arm and solemnly shook hands with himself.

KID CARDULA
by Jack Ritchie

Vampire stories may have their origins in the strange behavior of cliff dwellers who were bitten by rabid bats. But whatever gave them their start, it is a fact that vampire tales are still very popular today. All such yarns have "bite." However, we have found one that provides a knockout, too.

It's just about time for me to close down the gym for the night when this tall stranger comes up to me.

He wears a black hat, black suit, black shoes, black topcoat, and he carries a zipper bag.

His eyes are black too. "I understand that you manage boxers?"

I shrug. "I had a few good boys in my time."

Sure, I had a few good boys, but never *real* good. The best I ever done was with Chappie Strauss. He was listed as number ten in the lightweight division by *Ring Magazine*. Once. And I had to pick my fights careful to get him that far. Then he meets Galanio, which is a catastrophe, and he loses his next four fights too before I decide it's time to retire him.

"I would like you to manage me," the stranger says. "I plan to enter the fight ring."

I look him over. He seems well built and I put his weight at around one-ninety. Height maybe six foot one. But he looks pale, like his face hasn't seen the sun for some time. And there is also the question of his age. It's hard to pin-point, but he's no kid.

"How old are you?" I ask.

He shifts a little. "What is the ideal age for a boxer?"

"Mister," I say, "in this state it's illegal for any man over forty to even step into the ring."

"I'm thirty," he says fast. "I'll see that you get a birth certificate to verify that."

I smile a little. "Look, man, at thirty in this game, you're just about over the hill. Not starting."

His eyes glitter a little. "But I am strong. Incredibly strong."

I stretch the smile to a grin. "Like the poet says, you got the strength of ten because your heart is pure?"

He nods. "I do literally have the strength of ten, though not for that reason. As a matter of fact, realizing that I possessed this tremendous strength, it finally occurred to me that I might as well capitalize on it. Legitimately."

He puts down the zipper bag and walks over to where a set of barbells is laying on the mat and does a fast clean and jerk like he was handling a baby's rattle.

I don't know how many pounds is on that bar, weight lifting not being my field. But I remember seeing Wisniewski working with those weights a couple of hours ago and he grunts and sweats and Wisniewski is a heavyweight with a couple of state lifting titles to his credit.

I'm a little impressed, but still not too interested. "So you're strong. Maybe I can give you the names of a few of the weightmen who work out here. They got some kind of a club."

He glares, at which he seems good. "There is no money in weight lifting and I need a great deal of money." He sighs. "The subject of money never really entered my mind until recently. I simply dipped into my capital when necessary and then suddenly I woke one evening to discover that I was broke."

I look him over again. His clothes look expensive, but a touch shabby, like they been worn too long and maybe slept in.

"I do read the newspapers," he says, "including the sports pages, and I see that there is a fortune to be made in the prize ring with a minimum of effort." He indicates the zipper bag. "Before I ran completely out of money, I bought boxing trunks and shoes. I will have to borrow the boxing gloves."

I raise an eyebrow. "You mean you want to step into the ring with somebody right now?"

"Precisely."

I look down the gym floor. By now the place is empty except for Alfie Bogan, who's still working out on the heavy bag.

Alfie Bogan is a good kid and a hard worker. He's got a fair punch and high hopes for the ring. So far he's won all six of his fights, three by knockouts and three by decisions. But I can see what's in his future. He just don't have enough to get to the top.

All right, I think to myself. Why not give the gentleman in black a tryout and get this over with so I can get to bed, which is a cot in my office.

I call Alfie over and say, "This here nice man wants to step into the ring with you for a couple of rounds."

It's okay with Alfie, so the stranger disappears into the locker room and comes back wearing black trunks.

I fit him with gloves and he and Alfie climb into the ring and go to opposite corners.

I take the wrapper off a new cigar, stroke the gong, and start lighting up.

Alfie comes charging out of his corner, the way he always does, and meets the stranger three-quarters of the way across the ring. He throws a right and a left hook, which the stranger shrugs off. Then the stranger flicks out his left. You don't really see it, you just know it happened. It connects with Alfie's chin and Alfie hits the canvas on his back and stays there. I mean he's out.

I notice that my match is burning my fingers and quick blow it out. Then I climb into the ring to look at Alfie. He's still breathing, but he won't be awake for a while.

When you been in the fight game as long as I have, you don't need no long study to rate a fighter. Just that one left—and even the *sound* of it connecting—has got my heart beating a little faster.

I look around the gym for somebody to replace Alfie, but like I said before, it's empty. I lick my lips. "Kid, what about your right hand? Is it anywhere near as good as your left?"

"Actually my right hand is the better of the two."

I begin to sweat with the possibilities. "Kid, I'm impressed by your punch. I'll admit that. But the fight game is more than just punching. Can you *take* a punch too?"

He smiles thin—like a kid wearing new braces. "Of course. Please hit me."

Why not? I think. I might as well find out right now if he can take a punch. I take the glove off Alfie's right hand and slip into it.

In my day—which was thirty years ago—I had a pretty good right and I think I still got most of it. So I haul off and give it all I got. Right on the button of his chin.

And then I hop around the ring with tears in my eyes because I think I just busted my hand, but the stranger is still standing there with that narrow smile on his face and his hair not even mussed.

Alfie comes back into this world while I'm checking my hand and am relieved to discover that it ain't broken after all.

He groans and staggers to his feet, ready to start all over again. "A lucky punch." The boy is all heart, but no brains.

"No more tonight, Alfie," I say. "Some other time." I send him off to the showers and take the stranger into my office. "What's your name?"

"I am known as Cardula."

Cardula? Probably Puerto Rican, I guess. He's got a little accent. "All right," I say, "from now on you're Kid Cardula. Call me Manny." I light my cigar. "Kid, I just *may* be able to make something out of you. But first, let's get off on the right foot by making everything legal. First thing tomorrow morning we see my lawyer and he'll draw up papers which make us business associates."

Kid Cardula looks uneasy. "Unfortunately I can't make it tomorrow morning. Or the afternoon. For that matter, I can't make it *any* morning or afternoon."

I frown. "Why not?"

"I suffer from what may be termed photophobia."

"What's photophobia?"

"I simply cannot endure sunlight."

"You break out in a rash or something?"

"Quite a bit more than a rash."

I chew my cigar. "Does this photophobia hurt your fighting any?"

"Not at all. Actually I regard it as responsible for my strength. However all of my matches will have to be scheduled for evenings."

"Not much sweat there. Damn near all matches today are in the evening anyway." I think a little while. "Kid, I don't think we need to mention this photophobia to the State Medical Commission. I don't know how they stand on the subject and it's better we take no chances. This photophobia isn't catching, is it?"

"Not in the usual sense." He smiles wide this time, and I see why he's been smiling tight before. He's got these two outsize upper teeth, one on each side of his mouth. Personally, if I had teeth like that, I'd have them pulled, whether they got cavities or not.

He clears his throat. "Manny, would it be at all possible for me to get an advance on my future earnings?"

Ordinarily if anybody I just meet for the first time asks me for money, I tell him to forget it. But with Kid Cardula and his future, I think I can make an exception. "Sure, Kid," I say. "I guess you're a little short on eating money?"

"I am not particularly concerned about eating money," the Kid says. "But my landlord threatens to evict me if I don't pay the rent."

The next morning at around eleven, I get a phone call from Hanahan. It's about the McCardle-Jabloncic main event on Saturday night's card at the arena.

McCardle is Hanahan's pride and joy. He's a heavyweight, got some style and speed, and he's young. Hanahan is bringing him along careful, picking and choosing. Maybe McCardle isn't exactly championship material, but he should get in a few big money fights before it's time to retire.

"Manny," Hanahan says, "we got a little trouble with the Saturday night card. Jabloncic showed up at the weigh-ins with a virus, so he got scratched. I need somebody to fill in. You got anybody around there who'll fit the role?"

Jabloncic has 18 wins and 10 losses, which record don't

WATCHING OUT, HELPING OUT

THAT'S WHAT CRIME PREVENTION
IS ALL ABOUT

GSA LAW ENFORCEMENT BRANCH (9PX-3L)

look too bad on paper, except that it don't mention that he got six of them losses—all by knockouts—in a row after his eighteenth win. So I know exactly what type of a fighter Hanahan wants as a substitute for Jabloncic.

I think a little. Off hand, there are three or four veterans who hang around the gym and could use the money and don't mind the beating.

And then I remember Kid Cardula.

Ordinarily when you got a new boy, you bring him up slow, like three-round preliminaries. But with Kid Cardula I feel I got something that can't wait and we might as well take some shortcuts.

I speak into the phone. "Well, off hand, Hanahan, I can't think of anybody except this new face that just come to me last night. Kid Cardula, I think he calls himself."

"Never heard of him. What's his win-lose?"

"I don't know. He's some kind of foreign fighter. Puerto Rico, I think. I don't have his records yet."

Hanahan is cautious. "You ever seen him fight?"

"Well, I put him in the ring here for just a few seconds to see if he has anything. His left is fair, but I never seen him use his right hand once. Don't even know if he has one."

Hanahan is interested. "Anything else?"

"He came in here wearing a shabby suit and gave me a sob story about being down and out. He's thirty-five if he's a day. I'll swear to that."

Hanahan is pleased. "Well, all right. But I don't want anybody *too* easy. Can he stand up for a couple of rounds?"

"Hanahan, I can't guarantee anything, but I'll try the best I can."

That evening, when Kid Cardula shows up at the gym, I quick rush him to my lawyer and then to the weigh-in and physical under the arena, where I also sign papers which gives us ten percent of the night's gross.

I provide Kid Cardula with a robe which has got no lettering on the back yet, but it's black, his favorite color, and we go out into the arena.

McCardle is a local boy, which means he's got a following.

Half his neighborhood is at the arena and it ain't really a bad house. Not like the old days, but good enough.

We set up shop inside the ring and when the bell rings, McCardle makes the sign of the cross and dances out of his corner.

But Kid Cardula don't move an inch. He turns to me, and his face looks scared. "Does McCardle *have* to do that?"

"Do what?" I ask. "Now look, Kid, this is no time to get stage fright. Get out there and fight."

The Kid peeks back over his shoulder where the referee and McCardle are waiting for him in the center of the ring. Then he takes a deep breath, turns, and glides out of our corner.

His left whips out, makes the connection with McCardle's jaw, and it's all over. Just like that. McCardle is lying there in the same pose as Alfie Bogan last night.

Even the referee is stunned and wastes a few seconds getting around to the count, not that it really matters. The bout is wrapped up in nineteen seconds, including the count.

There's some booing. Not because anybody thinks that McCardle threw the fight, but because everything went so quick with the wrong man winning and the fans figure they didn't get enough time for the price of their tickets.

When we're back in the dressing room, the first person who comes storming in is Hanahan, his face beet red. He glares at Kid Cardula and then drags me to a corner. "What are you trying to do to me, Manny?"

I am innocence. "Hanahan, I swear that was the luckiest punch I ever seen in my life."

"You're damn right it was a lucky punch. We'll have the re-match as soon as I can book the arena again."

"Re-match?" I rub my chin. "Maybe so, Hanahan, but in this event I feel that I got to protect the Kid's interests. It's like a sacred trust. So for the re-match, we make his cut of the gate sixty percent instead of ten, right?"

Hanahan is fit to explode, but he's got this black spot on his fighter's record and the sooner he gets it off, the better. So by the time we finish yelling at each other, we decide to split the purse fifty-fifty, which is about what I expect anyway.

A couple of nights later when I close up the gym and go to my office, I find the Kid sitting there watching the late show on my portable TV set. It's one of them Dracula pictures and he turns to another channel when I enter.

I nod. "Never could stand them vampire pictures myself either. Even in a movie, I like logic, and they ain't got no logic."

"No logic?"

"Right. Like when you start off with one vampire and he goes out and drinks somebody's blood and that turns his victim into a vampire too, right? So now there's *two* vampires. A week later, they both get hungry and go out and feed on two victims. Now you got *four* vampires. A week later them four vampires go out to feed and now you got *eight* vampires."

"Ah, yes," Kid Cardula says. "And at the end of twenty-one weeks, one would logically expect to have a total of 1,048,576 vampires?"

"About that. And at the end of thirty weeks or so, everybody on the face of the earth is a vampire, and a week later all of them starve to death because they got no food supply any more."

Kid Cardula smiles, showing them big teeth. "You've got a head on your shoulders, Manny. However, suppose that these fictitious vampires, realizing that draining *all* of the blood from their victims will turn them into vampires and thereby competitors, exercise a certain restraint instead? Suppose they simply take a sip, so to speak, from one person and a sip from the next, leaving their victims with just a slight anemia and lassitude for a few days, but otherwise none the worse for wear?"

I nod, turn down the TV volume, and get back to the fight business. "Now, Kid, I know that you'll be able to put Mc-Cardle away again in a few seconds, but we got to remember that fighting is also show biz. People don't pay good money for long to see twenty-second fights. We got to give the customers a performance that lasts a while. So when we meet McCardle again, I want you to carry him for a few rounds. Don't hit too hard. Make the match look even until say the fifth round and *then* put him away."

I light a cigar. "If we look too good, Kid, we'll have trouble getting opponents later and we got to think about the future. A string of knockouts is fine, Kid, but don't make them look too easy."

In the weeks which follow while we're waiting for the McCardle re-match, I can't get the Kid to do any training at all—no road work and he won't even consider shadow boxing in front of a mirror.

So I leave it at that, not wanting to tamper with something that might be perfect. Also he won't give me his address. I suppose he's just got pride and don't want me to see the dump in which he lives. And he's got no phone. But he shows up at the gym every other night or so, just in case there's something concerning him.

The second McCardle fight comes and we take it in stride. The Kid carries McCardle for four rounds, but still making the bouts look good, and then in the fifth round he puts McCardle away with a short fast right.

In the days which follow, we don't have any particular trouble signing up more fights because we'll take any bout which comes our way. With Kid Cardula, I know I don't have to nurse him along. Also, we decide on the strategy of letting the Kid get himself knocked down two, maybe three, times per fight. With this maneuver, we establish that while the Kid can hit, he ain't so good at taking a punch. Consequently every manager who's got a pug with a punch figures that his boy has got a good chance of putting the Kid away.

We get seven bouts in the next year, all of which the Kid wins by knockouts, of course, and we're drawing attention from other parts of the country.

Now that some money is beginning to come in, I expect the Kid to brighten up a little, which he does for about six months, but then I notice that he's starting to brood about something. I try to get him to tell me about it, but he just shakes his head.

Also, now that he's getting publicity, he begins to attract the broads. They really go for his type. He's polite to them and all that, and even asks them their addresses, but as far as I know he never follows up or pays them a visit.

One morning after we'd just won our tenth fight—a nine round knockout over Irv Watson, who was on the way down, but still a draw—and I'm sitting in my office dreaming about the day soon when I sell the gym or at least hire somebody to manage it, there's a knock at the door.

The dame which enters and stands there looking scared is about your average height and weight, with average looks, and wearing good clothes. She's got black hair and a nose that's more than it should be. In all, nothing to get excited about.

She swallows hard. "Is this where I can find Mr. Kid Cardula?"

"He drops in every now and then," I say. "But it's not a schedule. I never know when he'll turn up."

"Would you have his address?"

"No. He likes to keep that a secret."

She looks lost for a few seconds and then decides to tell me what brought her here. "About two weeks ago I drove out of state to see my aunt Harriet and when I came back, I got a late start and it got dark before I could make it home. I'm really not at all good with directions and it had been raining. I turned and turned, hoping that I'd find a road that looked familiar. Somehow I got on this muddy road and my car skidded right into a ditch. And I just couldn't get the car out. Finally I gave up and sat there, waiting for some car to pass, but there was no traffic at all. I couldn't even see a farmhouse light. I guess I finally fell asleep. I had the strangest dream, but I can't remember now exactly what it was, and when I woke, there was this tall distinguished looking man standing beside the open door of my car and staring down at me. He gave me quite a start at first, but I recovered and asked him if he'd give me a lift to someplace where I could get to a phone and call my father and have him send someone out to pick me up. His car was parked on the road and he drove me to a crossroads where there was a gas station open."

I notice that she's got what look like two big mosquito bites on one side of her throat.

She goes on. "Anyway, while I was making the phone call, he drove away before I could thank him or get his name. But

I kept thinking about . . ." She blushed. "Then last night while I was watching the late news, there were things about sports and a picture of Kid Cardula appeared on the TV screen, and immediately I knew that this must be the stranger who had driven me to the gas station. So I asked around and somebody told me that you were his manager and gave me the address of your gym. And I just thought I'd drop in and thank him in person."

I nod. "I'll pass the thanks on to the Kid the next time I see him."

She still stands there, thinking, and suddenly she brightens again. "Also I wanted to return something to him. A money clip. With one thousand dollars in it. It was found beside my car when the tow truck went to pull it out of the ditch."

Sure, I think. Some nice honest tow truck driver finds a thousand bucks on the ground and he doesn't put it in his own pocket. But I nod again. "So give me the thousand and I'll see that the Kid gets it."

She laughs a little. "Unfortunately I forgot to bring the money and the clip with me." She opens her purse and takes out a ball-point pen and some paper. "My name is Carrington. Daphne Carrington. I'll write the directions on how to get to our place. It's a bit complicated. We call it Carrington Eyrie. Perhaps you've heard of it? It was featured in *Stately Home and Formal Garden Magazine* last year. Mr. Cardula will have to come in person, of course. So that he can identify the clip."

When Kid Cardula drops in the next evening, I tell him about Daphne Carrington and give him the slip of paper she left.

The Kid frowns. "I didn't lose a thousand dollars. Besides, I never use a money clip."

I grin. "I thought not. But still she's willing to ante up a thousand bucks to meet you. Is any part of her story true?"

"Well . . . I *did* drive her to that filling station after I . . . after I found her asleep in the car."

"I didn't know you owned a car."

"I bought it last week. There are some places just too far to fly."

"What model is it?"

"A 1974 Volkswagen. The motor's in good condition, but the body needs a little work." He sits on the corner of my desk, his eyes thoughtful. "*She* was driving a Lincoln Continental."

"Don't worry about it, Kid. Pretty soon you'll be driving Lincoln Continentals too."

We begin spacing out our fights now. No bum-of-the-month stuff. Mostly because we're getting better quality opponents and also because it needs time and publicity to build up the interest and the big gates.

We win a couple more fights, which get television coverage, and the Kid should be happy, but he's still brooding.

And then one night he shows up in my office and he makes an announcement. "Manny, I'm getting married."

I'm a little astounded, but I see no threat. Lots of fighters are married. "Who's the lucky lady?"

"Daphne Carrington."

I think a while before the name connects. "You mean *that* Daphne Carrington?"

He nods.

I stare at him. "I hope you don't take this wrong, Kid, but the dame ain't exactly no Raquel Welch, even in the face department."

His chin gets stubborn. "She has a tremendous personality."

That I doubt too. "Kid," I say, "be honest with yourself. She just ain't your type."

"She soon will be."

Suddenly the nub of the situation seems to flash into my mind and I'm shocked. "Kid you're not marrying this dame for her money, are you?"

He blushes, or looks like he tried to. "Why not? It's been done before."

"But, Kid, you don't *have* to marry anybody for their money. You're going to have money of your own soon. Big money. Millions."

He looks away. "Manny, I have been getting letters from my relatives and many concerned friends. But especially relatives. It seems that they have heard, or been told, about my ring appearances. And they all point out—rather strongly—that for a man with my background, it is unthinkable that I should be appearing in a prize ring."

He still didn't look at me. "I have been thinking this over

for a long time, Manny, and I am afraid that they are right. I shouldn't be a boxer. Certainly not a professional. All of my family and all of my friends strongly disapprove. And, Manny, one must have one's own self-respect and the approval of one's peers if one wants to achieve any happiness in this world."

"Peers?" I say. "You mean like royalty? You a count or something? You got blue blood in your veins?"

"Occasionally." He sighs. "My relatives have even begun a collection to save me from destitution. But I cannot accept charity from relatives."

"But you don't mind marrying a dame for her money?"

"My dear Manny," he says. "Marrying a woman for her money is as good a reason as any. Besides it will enable me to quit the fight game."

We argue and argue and I beg him to think it over for a while, telling him what all that ring money could mean to him—and me.

Finally he seems to give in a little, and when he leaves, he at least promises to think it over for a while.

About a week passes. I don't hear from him and I'm a nervous wreck. Finally, at around ten-thirty one evening, Alfie Bogan comes into my office with an envelope.

Right away I get the feeling that the envelope should have a black border. My fingers tremble when I open it and read the note from Kid Cardula.

Dear Manny:
I sincerely regret the way things have turned out, but I am determined to quit the ring. I know that you pinned a great deal of hope on my future and I am certain that, under different circumstances, we would have made those millions you talked about.

But goodbye and good luck. I have, however, decided not to leave you empty handed.

Best wishes,
Kid Cardula

Not leave me empty handed? Did he enclose a nice little check? I shake the envelope, but nothing comes out. What did he mean he wouldn't leave me empty handed?

I glare at Alfie Bogan, who's still standing there.

He grins. "Hit me."

I stare. Somehow Alfie looks different. He has these two big mosquito bites on his throat and these two long upper teeth, which I swear I never seen before.

"Hit me," he says again.

Maybe I shouldn't do it, but it's been a long hard week of disappointments. So I let him have it with all I got.

And break my hand.

But I'm smiling when the doc puts on the cast.

I got me a replacement for Kid Cardula.

THE MAN FROM P.I.G.
by Harry Harrison

As we shall see in a later story by Will Gray, genetic manipulation may one day make it possible to change animals. And while pigs might not seem the most likely candidates for such treatment, Harry Harrison makes a good case for "super pigs" in the following story, which could easily have been titled, "The Shoats Heard Round the World."

"This is the end of our troubles, Governor, it sure is!" the farmer said. The rustic next to him nodded agreement and was moved enough by the thought to lift the hat from his head, shout *yippee* once, then clamp it back on.

"Now I can't positively promise anything," Governor Haydin said, but there was more than a hint of eagerness in his words and he twirled his moustache with extraordinary exuberance. "Don't know any more about this than you do. We radioed for help and the Patrol said they'd do something . . ."

"And now a starcruiser is in orbit up there and her tender is on the way down," the farmer broke in, finishing the governor's sentence. "Sounds good enough for me. Help is on the way!"

The heavens boomed an answer to his words, and a spike of brilliant flame burned through the low-lying clouds above the field as the stubby form of the tender came into view. The crowd along the edge, almost the entire population of Trowbri City, burst into a ragged cheer. They restrained themselves as the ship rode its fiery exhaust down to the muddy field, settling in a cloud of steam, but as soon as the jets flicked off they surged forward to surround it.

"What's in there, Governor," someone asked, "a company of space commandos or suchlike?"

"The message didn't say—just asked for a landing clearance."

There was a hushed silence as the gangway ground out of its slot below the port and the end clattered down into the mud. The outer hatch swung open with the shrill whine of an electric motor and a man stepped into the opening and looked down at the crowd.

"Hi," he said, then turned and waved inside. "C'mon out, you-all," he shouted, then put his fingers to his lips and whistled shrilly.

His words evoked a chorus of high-pitched cries and squeals from inside the tender, and out of the port and down the gangway swept a thundering wave of animals. Their backs, pink, black and white, and gray, bobbed up and down and their hooves beat out a rumble of sound on the perforated metal.

"Pigs," the governor shouted, his angry voice rising over the chorus of porcine squeals. "Is there nothing but *pigs* aboard this ship?"

"There's me, sir," the man said, stopping in front of the governor. "Wurber's my name, Bron Wurber, and these here are my animals. I'm mighty glad to meet you."

Governor Haydin's eyes burnt a track up from the ground, slowly consuming every inch of the tall man who stood before him, taking in the high rubber boots, the coarse material of the crumpled trousers, the heavy, stained folds of the once-red jacket, the wide smiling face and clear blue eyes of the pig farmer. The governor winced when he saw the bits of straw in the man's hair. He completely ignored Wurber's outstretched hand.

"What are you doing here?" Haydin asked.

"Come to homestead. Figure to open me a pig ranch. It'll be the only pig ranch for more'n fifty light-years in any direction and, not meaning to boast, that's saying a lot." He wiped his right hand on his jacket then slowly extended it again. "Name's Wurber, most folk call me Bron because that's my first name. I'm afraid I didn't catch yours?"

"Haydin," he said, reluctantly extending his hand. "I'm

the governor here." He looked down abstractedly at the rounded, squealing forms that milled about them in a churning circle.

"Why I'm that pleased to meet you, Governor, it's sure a big job you got here," Bron said, happily pumping the other's hand up and down.

The rest of the spectators were already leaving and when one of the pigs, a great, rounded sow, came too close to them a man turned and lashed out an iron-shod boot. Her shrill screams sliced the air like a run-wild buzz saw as she fled.

"Here, none of that," Bron shouted over the backs of his charges. The angry man just shook his fist backwards and went away with the rest of the crowd.

"Clear the area," an amplified voice bellowed from the tender. "Blast off in one minute. Repeat, sixty seconds to blast-off."

Bron whistled again and pointed to a grove of trees at the edge of the field. The pigs squealed answer and began moving in that direction. The trucks and cars were pulling out and when the churning herd—with Bron and the governor at its center—reached the edge of the field only the governor's car was left. Bron started to say something but his words were drowned out by the tender's rockets and the deafening squealing and grunting of fright that followed it. When it died away he spoke again.

"If you're driving into the city, sir, I wonder if you'd let me drive along with you. I have to file my land claims."

"You wouldn't want to do that," the governor said, groping around for an excuse to get rid of the rustic clod. "This herd is valuable property, you wouldn't want to leave them here alone."

"Do you mean there're criminals and *thieves* in your town?"

"I didn't say that," Haydin snapped. "The people here are as decent and law abiding as any you can find. It's just that, well, we're a little short of meat animals and the sight of all that fresh pork on the hoof . . ."

"Why that notion is plumb criminal, Governor. This is the finest breeding stock that money can buy and none of them are for slaughtering. Do you realize that every critter here will eventually be the ancestor of entire herds of . . ."

"Just spare me the lecture on animal husbandry, I'm needed in the city."

"Can't keep the good folks waiting," Bron said with a wide and simple smile. "I'll drive in with you and make my own way back. I'm sure these swine will be safe enough here. They can root around in this patch of woods and take care of themselves for a bit."

"Well it's your funeral—or maybe theirs," Haydin mumbled, getting into the electric car and slamming the door behind him. He looked up with a sudden thought as Bron climbed in the other side. "Say . . . where's your luggage? Did you forget it in the tender?"

"Now that's shore nice of you to worry about me like that." Bron pointed out at the herd which had separated a bit now that the swine were rooting happily in the forest humus. A large boar had two long cases strapped to his back, and a smaller pig nearby had a battered suitcase tied on at a precarious angle.

"People don't appreciate how all-around valuable pigs are. On Earth they've been beasts of burden for umpteen thousands of years, yessir. Why there's nothing as all-around as a pig. The old Egyptians used them for planting seeds, you know their bitty little sharp hooves just trod those seeds down to the right depth in the soft soil."

Governor Haydin jammed the rheostat full on and drove numbly into town with a bucolic discourse on swinology echoing about his head. Bron followed him into the municipal building and the governor quickly turned him over to his aide, Lea Davies, who, along with the banks of computers, made up the complete governmental staff. She was putting her handkerchief away as they came up, and her eyes were red. The governor gave her shoulder a quick pat before vanishing into his office.

Bron filed his claim papers and obtained maps of the areas opened to homesteading. Lea was businesslike and efficient but could not be led into a discussion about anything other than the matter at hand. Bron finally promised to return and make a detailed claim as soon as he had looked over the various parcels of land. He stumped out, clumsy in his heavy boots, and stood on the top of the steps looking down Trowbri City's main—and almost only—street.

Prefabs and pressure huts were interspersed with rammed earth buildings and woodframe structures. Trowbri had only been colonized for a few years and was still in its raw and vigorous youth. The city was also the planet's only settlement, though farms and small factories trickled out into the surrounding countryside. This was a good planet, like Earth in many ways, fertile and plump with mineral wealth waiting to be tapped. The settlers had all been hand chosen and were well financed; it should have been a happy place. Instead there was an undefinable feeling of unease in the air, a look on the faces of the passersby, the obvious fact that Lea Davies had been crying yet would not talk about it.

Hands in pockets, whistling lightly through his teeth, Bron walked back slowly to the spaceport—really just a cleared area and control tower—looking about him as he went.

As he came near the grove where he had left his animals he heard a shrill, angry squealing. He quickened his pace, then broke into a ground-consuming run as other squeals joined the first. Some of the pigs were still rooting unconcernedly, but most of them were gathered about a tall tree that was entwined with creepers and studded with short branches. A boar reared his head out of the milling herd and slashed at the tree, peeling away a yard long strip of bark. From high in the tree a hoarse voice called for help.

Bron whistled instructions, pulled on tails and pushed on fat flanks and finally got the pigs moving about again. As soon as they began rooting and stripping the berries from the bushes he called up into the tree.

"Whoever's there can come down now. It's safe."

The tree shook and a patter of bits of bark fell, and a tall, skinny man climbed down slowly into view. He stopped above Bron's head, holding tightly to the trunk. His trousers were torn and the heel was gone from one boot.

"Who are you?" Bron asked.

"Are these your beasts?" the man said angrily. "They ought to be shot. They attacked me, viciously . . . would have killed me if I hadn't got to this tree . . ."

"Who are you?" Bron repeated.

". . . Vicious and uncontrolled. If you don't take care of them, I will. We have laws here on Trowbri . . ."

"If you don't shut up and tell me who you are, mister, you can just stay in that tree until you rot," Bron said quietly. He pointed to the large boar who was lying down about ten feet from the tree and glaring at it out of tiny, red eyes. "I don't have to do anything and these pigs will take care of you all by themselves. It's in their blood. Peccaries in Mexico will tree a man and then take turns standing guard below until he dies, or falls out. These animals here don't attack anyone without reason. I say the reason is you came by and tried to grab up one of the sucklings because you had a sudden yearning for fresh pork. Who are you?"

"You calling me a liar?" the man shouted.

"Yes. Who are you?"

The boar came over and butted against the tree and made a deep grumbling noise. The man above clutched the tree with both arms and all the air went out of him.

"I'm . . . Reymon . . . the radio operator here. I was in the tower landing the tender. When it left I grabbed my cycle and started back to town. I saw these pigs here and I stopped, just to have a look, and that's when I was attacked. Without reason . . ."

"Shore, shore," Bron said, and dug his toe into the boar's side and scraped it up and down on the heavy ribs. The boar flapped his ears and rumbled a happy grunt. "You like it up in that tree, Mr. Reymon?"

"All right then, I bent down to touch one of your filthy animals. Don't ask me why. Then I was attacked."

"That sounds more like it, and I'm not gonna bother you with foolish questions as to why you had a sudden urge to pet a filthy pig. You can come down now and get on your red wagon and get moving."

The boar flicked its twist of a tail, then vanished into the undergrowth. Reymon shakily dropped to the ground and brushed off his clothes. He was a darkly handsome man whose features were spoiled by the angry tightness of his mouth.

"You'll hear more about this," he said over his shoulder as he stumbled away.

"I doubt it," Bron told him. He went to the road and waited until the electrobike whizzed by in the direction of the city. Only then did he go back and whistle his flock together.

It was well past midnight, much closer to dawn, when the shadow slid across the street and slipped behind the municipal building. It moved close to the ground, a tiny dark shape that was almost impossible to see. A moment later a taller form joined it. One of the windows slid open soundlessly and the shadows vanished from sight. The night sounds started up again in the surrounding bushes.

Governor Haydin sat up suddenly as the lights came on in his bedroom. The first thing he saw was a small pink pig sitting on the rug by his bed. It turned its head to look him directly in the eye—then winked. It had lovely, long white eyelashes.

"Sorry to disturb you at this hour," Bron said from the window, as he made sure the curtains were completely drawn, "but I didn't want anyone to see us meeting."

"Get out of here you insane swineherd before I throw you out!" Haydin bellowed.

"Not so loud, sir," Bron cautioned. "You may be overheard. Here is my identification." He held out a plastic rectangle.

"I know who you are, so what difference . . ."

"Not this identification. You did ask the Patrol for aid on this planet, didn't you?"

"What do you know about that?" The governor's eyes widened at the thought. "You mean to say you have something to do with them?"

"My identification," Bron said, snapping to attention and handing over the card.

Governor Haydin grabbed it with both hands. "P.I.G." he read. "What's that?" Then answered his own question in a hoarse voice as he read the next line. "*Porcine Interstellar Guard!* Is this some kind of joke?"

"Not at all, Governor. The Guard has only been recently organized and activated while knowledge of its activities has heretofore been confined to command levels, where its operational configurations are top secret."

"All of a sudden you don't sound like a pig farmer any more."

"I am a pig farmer, Governor. But I have a degree in animal husbandry, a doctorate in galactic politics and a black belt in judo. The pig farmer is used for field cover."

"Then—*you're* the answer to my distress message to the Patrol?"

"That's correct. I can't give you any classified details, but you must surely know how thin the Patrol is spread these days— and will be for years to come. When a new planet is opened up it extends Earth's sphere of influence in a linear direction—but the volume of space that must be controlled is the *cube* of that distance. The Patrol must operate between all the planets and the volume of space that this comprises is beyond imagining. Someday, it is hoped, there will be enough Patrol vessels to fill this volume so that a cruiser can answer any call for help. But as it stands now, other means of assistance must be found. There are a number of projects being instigated and the P.I.G. is one of the first to go operational. You've seen my unit. We can travel by any form of commercial transportation so we can operate without Patrol assistance. We carry rations, but if needs be are self-supporting. We are equipped to handle almost any tactical situation."

Haydin was trying to understand but it was still all too much for him. "I hear what you're saying, still," he faltered, "all you have is a herd of pigs."

Bron grabbed his temper hard and his eyes narrowed to slits with the effort. "Would you have felt better if I had landed with a pack of wolves? Would that have given you some sense of security?"

"Well, I do admit that it would look a good deal different. I could see some sense in that."

"Can you? In spite of the fact that in their natural state a wolf—or wolves—will run from a full-grown wild boar without ever considering attacking him. And I have a mutated boar out there that will take on any six wolves and produce six torn wolf skins in about as many minutes. Do you doubt this?"

"It's not a matter of doubt. But you have to admit that there is something . . . I don't know . . . ludicrous maybe, about a herd of pigs."

"That observation is not exactly original," Bron said in a toneless, arctic voice. "In fact that is the reason I take the whole herd rather than just boars, and why I do the dumb farmer bit. People take no notice and it helps my investigation. Which is also why I am seeing you at night like this. I don't want to blow my cover until I have to."

"That's one thing you won't have to worry about. Our problem doesn't involve any of the settlers."

"What exactly *is* your problem? Your message wasn't exactly clear on that point."

Governor Haydin looked uncomfortable. He wriggled a bit, then examined Bron's identification again. "I'll have to check this before I can tell you anything."

"Please do."

There was a fluoroscope on the end table and Haydin made a thorough job of comparing the normally invisible pattern with the code book he took from his safe. Finally, almost reluctantly, he handed the card back. "It's authentic," he said.

Bron slipped the card back into his pocket. "Now what is the trouble?" he asked.

Haydin looked at the small pig that was curled up on the rug, snoring happily. "It's ghosts," he said in a barely audible voice.

"And you're the one who laughs at pigs."

"There's no need to get offensive," the governor answered warmly. "I know it sounds strange, but there it is. We call them —or the phenomena—'ghosts' because we don't know whether they're supernatural or not. It's anyone's guess, but it's sure not physical." He turned to the map on the wall and tapped a yellowish-tan area that stood out from the surrounding green.

"Right here, the Ghost Plateau, that's where the trouble is."

"What sort of trouble?"

"It's hard to say, just a feeling mostly. Ever since this planet was settled, going on fifteen years now, people haven't liked to go near the plateau, even though it lies almost outside the city. It doesn't feel right up there, somehow. Even the animals stay away. And people have disappeared there and no trace has ever been found of them."

Bron looked at the map, tracing the yellow gradient outline with his finger. "Hasn't it been explored?" he asked.

"Of course, in the first survey. And copters still fly over it and there's never anything out of the way to be seen. But only in daylight. No one has ever flown, or driven, or walked on the Ghost Plateau during the night and lived to tell about it. Nor has a single body ever been found."

The governor's voice was heavy with grief: there was no doubt that he meant what he said. "Has anything ever been done about this?" Bron asked.

"Yes. We've learned to stay away. This is not Earth, Mr. Wurber, no matter to how many points it resembles it. It is an alien planet with alien life on it, and this human settlement is just a pinprick in the planet's hide. Who knows what . . . creatures are out there in the night. We are settlers, not adventurers. We have learned to avoid the plateau, at least at night, and we have never had that kind of trouble anywhere else."

"Then why have you called on the Patrol?"

"Because we made a mistake. The old-timers don't talk much about the plateau and a lot of the newcomers believe that the stories are just . . . stories. Some of us even began to doubt our own memories. In any case, a prospecting team wanted to look for some new mine sites, and the only untouched area near the city is on the plateau. In spite of our misgivings the team went out, led by an engineer name of Huw Davies."

"Any relation to your assistant?"

"Her brother."

"That explains her agitation. What happened?"

Haydin's eyes were unfocused as he gazed at a fearful

memory. "It was horrible," he said. "We took all precautions, of course, followed them by copter during the day and marked their camp. The copters were rigged with lights and we stood by all night. They had three radios and all of them were in use so there could be no communication breakdown. We waited all night and there was no trouble. Then, just before dawn— without any alarm or warning—the radios cut out. We got there within minutes, but it was too late. What we found is almost too awful to describe. Everything—their equipment, tents, supplies—was destroyed, crushed and destroyed. There was blood everywhere, spattering the broken trees and the ground—but the men were gone, vanished. There were no tracks of animals, or men, or machines in the area—nothing. The blood was tested, it was human blood. And the fragments of flesh were . . . human flesh."

"There must have been something," Bron insisted. "Some identifying marks, some clues, perhaps the odor of explosive, or something on your radar since this plateau is so close."

"We are not stupid men. We have technicians and scientists. There were no clues, no smells, nothing on radar. I repeat, nothing."

"And this is when you decided to call the Patrol."

"Yes. This thing is too big for us to handle."

"You were absolutely correct, Governor. I'll take it from here. In fact I already have a very good idea what happened."

Haydin was jolted to his feet. "You can't! What is it?"

"I'm afraid it is a little too early to say. I'm going up to the plateau in the morning to look at this place where the massacre happened. Can you give me the map coordinates? And please don't mention my visit to anyone."

"Little chance of that," Haydin said, looking at the little pig. It stood and stretched, then sniffed loudly at the bowl of fruit on the table.

"Jasmine would like a piece," Bron said. "You don't mind, do you?"

"Go ahead, help yourself," the governor said resignedly, and loud chomping filled the room as he wrote down the coordinates and directions.

There was little of the night left and the animals were up and stirring about when Bron came back to the camp.

"I think we'll stay here at least another day," he said as he cracked open a case of vitamin rations. Queeny, the eight-hundred-pound Poland China sow, grunted happily at this announcement and rooted up a wad of leaves and threw them into the air.

"Good foraging, I don't doubt it, particularly after all that time in the ship. I'm going to take a little trip, Queeny, and I'll be back by dark. You keep an eye on things until then." He raised his voice, "Curly! Moe!"

A crashing in the forest echoed his words and a moment later two long, grayish-black forms tore out of the underbrush, a ton of bone and muscle on the hoof. A three-inch branch was in Curly's way and he neither swerved nor slowed. There was a sharp crack and he skidded up to Bron with the broken branch draped across his back. Bron threw the branch aside and looked at his shock troops.

They were boars, twins from the same litter, and weighed over one thousand pounds apiece. An ordinary wild boar will weigh up to seven hundred fifty pounds and is the fastest, most dangerous and bad-tempered beast known. Curly and Moe were mutants, a third again heavier and many times as intelligent as their wild ancestors. But nothing else had changed. They were still just as fast, dangerous and bad tempered, only they weighed a good deal more and their ten-inch tusks were capped with tough plastic to prevent them from splitting.

"I want you to stay here with Queeny, Moe, and she'll be in charge."

Moe squealed in anger and tossed his great head. Bron grabbed a handful of hide and thick bristles between Moe's shoulder blades, the boar's favorite itch spot, and twisted and pummeled it. Moe burbled happily through his nose. Moe was a pig genius, which made him a sort of retarded moron on the human level—except he wasn't human. He understood simple orders and would obey them within the limits of his capacity.

"Stay and guard, Moe, stay and guard. Watch Queeny, she knows what is best. Guard, don't kill. Plenty good things to eat here—and candy when I get back. Curly goes with me, and everyone gets candy when we come back." There were happy grunts from all sides and Queeny pressed her fat side against his leg.

Bron used his compass to get a heading towards the Ghost Plateau and pointed his arm in the correct direction. Curly put his head down and catapulted into the undergrowth. There was a snapping and crackling as he tore his way through, the perfect pathfinder who made his own openings where none were available.

"You, too, Jasmine," Bron said. "A good walk will keep you out of trouble. Go get Maisie Mule-Foot, the exercise will do her good, too."

Jasmine was his problem child. Though she only looked like a half-grown shoat, she was a full grown Pitman-Moore miniature, a strain of small pigs that had originally been developed for use in laboratories. This breed had been used in breeding for intelligence and Jasmine probably had the highest I.Q. ever to come out of the lab. But there was a handicap; with the intelligence went an instability, an almost human hysteria as though her mind were balanced on a sharp edge. If she were left with the other pigs she would tease and torture them and cause trouble, so Bron made sure that she was with him if he had to be away from the herd for any length of time.

Maisie was a totally different case, a typical, well-rounded sow, a Mule-Foot, a general purpose breed. Her intelligence was low—or pig-normal—and her fecundity high. Some cruel people might say she was good only for bacon. But she had a pleasant personality and was a good mother; in fact she had just been weaned from her last litter. Bron took her along to give her some relief from her weanling progeny—and also to run some fat off her since she had grown uncommonly plump during the confined space voyage.

They made good time, in spite of Maisie's wheezing complaints, and within an hour had reached the rising ground that marked the approach to the plateau. There was a stream here and Bron let the pigs drink their fill while he cut himself a stick for the climb. Maisie, overheated by her exertions, dropped full length into the water with a tremendous splash and soaked herself. Jasmine, a fastidious animal, squealed with rage and rushed away to roll in the grass and dry herself off where she had been splashed. Curly, with much chuffing and grunting like a satisfied locomotive, got his nose under a rotting log that must have weighed over a half ton and rolled it over and happily consumed the varied insect and animal life he found beneath it. They moved on.

It was not a long climb to the plateau, and once over the edge the ground leveled out into a lightly forested plain. Bron took another compass reading and pointed Curly in the right direction. He snorted and raked a furrow in the ground with a forehoof before setting off, and Jasmine pressed up against Bron's leg and squealed. Bron could feel it, too, and had to suppress an involuntary shiver. There was something—how could it be described?—*wrong* about this place. He had no idea why he felt this way, but he did. And the pigs seemed to sense it, too. There was something else wrong, there was not a bird in sight although the hills below had been filled with them. And there did not seem to be any other animals about; the pigs would surely have called his attention to any he might have missed.

Bron fought down the sensation and followed Curly's retreating hindquarters, while the two other pigs, still protesting, trotted behind him, staying as close to his legs as possible. It was obvious that they all felt this presentiment of danger, and they were all bothered by it. All except Curly, that is, since any strange emotion or sensation just tripped his boarish temper so that he plowed ahead filled with mumbling anger.

When they reached the clearing there was no doubt that it was the correct one. Branches on all sides were bent and twisted and small trees pulled down, while torn tents and crushed equipment littered the area. Bron picked up a transceiver and saw that the metal case had been pinched and twisted, as though squeezed by some giant hand.

And all of the time, as he searched the area, he was aware of the tension and pressure.

"Here, Jasmine," he said, "take a smell of this. I know it's been out in the rain and sun for weeks now, but there may be a trace of something left. Give a sniff."

Jasmine shivered and shook her head *no* and pressed up against his legs: he could feel her body shiver. She was in one of her states and good for nothing until it passed. Bron didn't blame her—he felt a little that way himself. He gave Curly the case to smell, and the boar took an obliging sniff, but his attention wasn't really on it. His little eyes scanned in all directions while he smelled it, and then he sniffed around the clearing, snuffling and snorting to blow the dirt out of his nostrils. Bron thought he was on to something when he began to rip the ground with his upper tusks, but it was only a succulent root that he had smelled. He chomped at it—then suddenly raised his head and pointed his ears at the woods, the root dangling forgotten from his jaws.

"What is it?" Bron asked, because the other two animals were pointing in the same direction, listening intently. Their ears twitched and there was the sudden sound of something large crashing through the bush.

The suddenness of the attack almost finished Bron. The crashing still sounded some distance away when the Bounder plunged out of the woods almost on top of him, foot-long yellow claws outstretched. Bron had seen pictures of these giant marsupials, native to the planet, but the reality was something else again. It stood on its hind legs, twelve feet high, and even the knowledge that it was not carnivorous and used the claws for digging in the marshes was not encouraging. It also used them against its enemies and he seemed to be in that category at the moment. The creature sprang out, loomed over him, the claws swung down.

Curly, growling with rage, hit the beast from the side. Even twelve feet of brown-furred marsupial cannot stand up to one thousand pounds of angry boar and the big beast went over and back. As he passed, Curly flicked his head with a wicked twist that hooked a tusk into the animal's leg and ripped. With a lightning spin the boar reversed direction and returned to the attack.

The Bounder was not having any more. Shrieking with pain and fear it kept on going in the opposite direction just as its mate—the one that had been blundering through the woods—appeared in the clearing. Curly spun again, reversing within one body length, and charged. The Bounder, it must have been the male because of its size, sized the situation up instantly and did not like it. Its mate was fleeing in pain—and telling everybody about it loudly—and without a doubt this underslung, hurtling mass of evil-looking creature must be to blame. Without slowing the Bounder kept going and vanished among the trees on the opposite side.

Through the entire affair Jasmine had rushed about, accomplishing very little but obviously on the verge of a nervous breakdown. Maisie, never one for quick reflexes, just stood and flapped her ears and grunted with amazement.

As Bron reached into his pocket to get a Miltown for Jasmine the long, green snake slithered out of the woods almost at his feet.

He stopped, frozen, with his hand halfway to his pocket, because he knew he was looking at death. This was the Angelmaker, the most poisonous serpent on Trowbri, more deadly than anything mother Earth had ever produced. It had the meat-hungry appetite of a constrictor—because it was a constrictor in its eating habits—but it also had fangs and well-filled venom sacks. And it was agitated, weaving back and forth and preparing to strike.

It was obvious that portly, pink Maisie, sow and mother, did not have the reflexes, or the temperament, to deal with attacking marsupials—but a snake was something else altogether. She squealed and jumped forward, moving her weight with ponderous agility.

The Angelmaker saw the appealing mass of quivering flesh and struck, instantly darting its head back and striking again. Maisie, snorting with the effort to turn her head and look back over her shoulder, squealed again and backed towards the poised snake. It hissed loudly and struck another time, perhaps wondering in some dim corner of its vestigial brain why this appealing dinner did not drop down so he could eat it. If the Angelmaker knew a bit more about pigs, it might have acted differently. Instead it struck again, and by now most of its venom was gone.

While the Mule-Foot is not a lard type, it is a sturdy breed and the females do run to fat. Maisie was plumper than most. Her hind quarters, what some crude carnivorous types might call her hams, were coated with heavy fat. And there is no blood circulation through fat. The venom was deposited in the fat where it could not reach the blood stream and could do no injury. Eventually it would be neutralized and disposed of. Right now Maisie was turning the tables. The Angelmaker struck again, listlessly, because its venom was gone. Maisie heaved her bulk about and chopped down with her hooves, strong, sharp-edged weapons. While snakes may like to kill pigs, pigs greatly enjoy eating snakes.

Squealing and bouncing heavily Maisie landed on the snake's spine and neatly amputated its head. The body still writhed and she attacked again, chopping with her hooves until the snake had been cut into a number of now motionless segments. Only then did she stop attacking and mumbled happily to herself while she ate them. It was a big snake and she allowed Curly and Jasmine to help her with it. Bron waited for them to finish before moving out, because the feast was calming them down. Only when the last chunk had vanished did he turn and start back for the camp. He kept looking back over his shoulder and found that it was a great relief—for all of them—to start down the slope away from the Ghost Plateau.

They were greeted with grunts of welcome when they reached the rest of the herd, while the most intelligent beasts remembered the promised candy and crowded around waiting for it. Bron opened a case of the vitamin and mineral reinforced candy and while he was distributing it he heard the buzz of his phone, very dimly because he had yet to unpack it from the carrying case. When he had filled out the homesteading forms he had entered his phone number, but as far as he knew the only person who had seen the papers was Lea Davies. He pulled out the phone, flipped up the screen and thumbed it on.

"Now I was just thinking 'bout you, Miss Davies," he said to the image on the small screen. "Ain't that a coincidence."

"Very," she said, barely moving her lips when she spoke, as though groping for words. She was a pretty girl, but looking too haggard now. Her brother's death had hit her hard. "I must see you . . . Mr. Wurber. As soon as possible."

"Now that's right friendly, Miss Lea, I'm looking forward to that."

"I need your help, but we mustn't be seen talking together. Can you come as soon as it is dark, alone, to the rear entrance of the municipal building? I'll meet you there."

"I'll be there—you can count on me," he said, and rung off.

What was this about? Did the girl know something no one else knew? It was possible. Then, too, the governor might have told her about P.I.G., since she was his only assistant. And on top of that she was very attractive, when she wasn't crying. As soon as he had fed the herd he broke out some clean clothes and his razor.

Bron left at dusk and Queeny lifted her head to watch him go. She would be in charge until he came back. The rest of the pigs knew and expected that, and she had Curly and Moe ready to take care of any trouble that might arise. Curly was sleeping off the day's exertions, whistling placidly through his nose, and next to him little Jasmine was also asleep, even more tired and sedated by a large Miltown. The situation was well in hand.

Approaching the municipal building from its unlighted rear was no problem, since he had been over the same ground just the previous evening. All this running about was getting to him at last and he choked off a yawn with his fist.

"Miss Lea, are you there?" he called softly, pushing open the unlocked door. The hall beyond was black, and he hesitated.

"Yes, I'm here," her voice called out. "Please come in."

Bron pushed the door wide, stepped through, and a crashing pain struck him across the side of the head, the agony of it lighting the darkness of his nerves for an instant. He tried to say something, but could not speak, though he did manage to raise his arm. Another blow struck his forearm, numbing it so that it dropped away, and the third blow across the back of his neck sent him plunging down into a deeper darkness.

"What happened?" the wavering pink blob asked, and with much blinking Bron managed to focus on it and recognized Governor Haydin's worried face.

"You tell me," Bron said hoarsely, and was aware for the first time of the pain in his head and he almost passed out again. Something damp and cool snuffled against his neck and he worked his hand up to twist Jasmine's ear.

"I thought I told you to get that pig out of here," someone said.

"Leave her be," Bron said, "and tell me what happened." He turned his head, with infinite caution, and saw that he was lying on the couch in the governor's office. A medical-looking type with a stern face and dangling stethoscope was standing by. There were a number of other people at the doorway.

"We just found you here," the governor said. "That's all we know. I was just leaving my office when I heard this screaming, like a girl getting her throat cut, something terrible. Some of these other men heard it outside in the street and we all came running. Found you lying in the rear hall, out cold with your head laid open, and this pig standing next to you doing all the screaming. I never knew an animal could sound like that. It wouldn't let anyone near you, kept charging and chomping its teeth in a very threatening manner. Quieted down a bit by the time the doctor came and finally let him get over to you."

Bron thought quickly, or at least as quickly as he could with a powersaw trying to take off the back of his head.

"Then you know as much about it as I do," he said. "I came here to see about filing my homesteading papers. The front was locked and I thought maybe I could get in by the back, if anyone was still here. I walked through the back door and something hit me and the next thing I knew I was waking up here. Guess I can thank Jasmine for that. She must have followed me and seen me hit. Must have started squealing, like you heard, and probably chewed on the ankle of whoever hit me. Pigs have very good teeth. Must have frightened off whoever it was." He groaned, "Can you give me something for my head?"

"There is a possibility of concussion," the doctor said.

"I'll take my chances on that, Doc, better a little concussion than my head splitting into two halves this way."

By the time the doctor had finished and the crowd dispersed his head had subsided to a throbbing ache, and Bron was fingering his bruised arm which he had just noticed for the first time. He waited until the governor had closed and locked the door before he spoke.

"I didn't tell you the whole story," he said.

"I didn't think you had. Now what is this all about?"

"I was struck by a party or parties unknown, that part was all true, and if Jasmine had not woke up and found me missing and gotten all neurotically insecure I would probably be dead at this moment. It was a trap and I walked into it."

"What do you mean?"

"I mean that Lea Davies is involved in this. She called me, arranged to meet me here and was waiting here when I arrived."

"Are you trying to say . . ."

"I've said it. Now get the girl in here so we can hear her side of it."

It took over an hour for Governor Haydin to prove to his own satisfaction that Lea had vanished. The settled portion of Trowbri covered a limited area and everyone could be reached by phone. No one had seen her, or knew where she was. She was gone. Bron had faced this fact long before the governor would admit it—and he knew what had to be done. He slumped back in the chair, half-dozing, with his shoes off and his feet propped on Jasmine's warm flank. The little pig was out like a light, sleeping the sleep of the just.

"She's gone," Haydin said, switching off the last call. "How can it be? She couldn't have had anything to do with your being attacked."

"She could have—if she were forced into it."

"What are you talking about?"

"I'm just guessing, but it makes sense. Suppose her brother is not dead . . ."

"What are you saying?"

"Let me finish. Suppose her brother is alive, but in deadly danger. And she had the chance to save him if she did as ordered—which was to get me here. Give the girl credit, I don't think she knew they meant to kill me. She must have put up a fight, that's why she was taken away, too."

"What do you know, Wurber?" Haydin shouted. "Tell me —everything. I'm governor here and I have a right to know."

"And know you shall—when I have anything more than hunches and guesses to give you. This attack, and the kidnapping, means that someone is unhappy about my presence, which also means that I am getting close. I'm going to speed things up and see if I can catch these 'ghosts' offguard."

"Do you think there is a connection between all this and the Ghost Plateau?"

"I *know* there is. That's why I want the word circulated in the morning that I am moving into my homestead tomorrow. Make sure everyone knows where it is."

"Where?"

"On the Ghost Plateau—where else?"

"That's suicide!"

"Not really. I have some guesses as to what happened up there, and some defenses—I hope. I also have my team, and they've proven themselves twice today. It will be taking a chance, but I'm going to have to take a chance if we ever hope to see Lea alive again."

Haydin clenched his fists on the desktop and made up his mind. "I can stop this if I want to—but I won't if you do it my way. Full radio connection, armed guards, the copters standing by . . ."

"No, sir, thank you very much but I remember what happened to the last bunch that tried it that way."

"Then—I'll go with you myself. I'm responsible for Lea. You'll take me, or you won't go."

Bron smiled. "Now that's a deal, Guv. I could use a helping hand, and maybe a witness. Things are going to get pretty busy on the plateau tonight. But no guns."

"That's suicide."

"Just remember the first expedition, and do it my way. I'm leaving most of my equipment behind. I imagine you can arrange to have it trucked to a warehouse until we get back. I think you'll find I have a good reason for what I'm doing."

Bron managed to squeeze in over ten hours sleep because he felt he was going to need it. By noon the truck had come and gone and they were on their way. Governor Haydin was dressed for the occasion, in hunting boots and rough clothes and he moved right out with them. Not that the pace was so fast, they went at the speed of the slowest piglet, and there was much noisy comment from all sides and grabbing of quick snacks from the roadside. They took the same course as the original expedition, a winding track that led up to the plateau in easy stages, for the most part running beside a fast river of muddy water. Bron pointed to it.

"Is this the river that runs through the plateau?" he asked.

Haydin nodded. "This is the one, it comes down from that range of mountains back there."

Bron nodded, then ran to rescue a squealing suckling from a crack in the rocks into which it had managed to wedge itself. They moved on.

By sunset they had set up camp—in the glade just next to the one where the previous expedition had met its end.

"Do you think this is a good idea?" Haydin asked.

"The best," Bron told him. "It's the perfect spot for our needs." He eyed the sun, which was close to the horizon. "Let's eat now, I want everything squared away by dark."

Bron had opened a tremendous tent, but it was sparsely furnished, two folding chairs and a battery-powered light to be exact.

"Isn't this a little on the spartan side?" Haydin asked.

"I see no reason to bring equipment forty-five light-years just to have it destroyed. We've obviously set up camp, that's all that's important. The equipment I need is in here." He tapped a small plastic sack that hung from his shoulder. "Now—chow's up."

Their table was an empty ration box that had held the pigs' dinner. A good officer always sees to his troops first, so the animals had been fed. Bron put two self-heating dinners on the box, broke their seals, and handed Haydin a plastic fork. It was almost dark by the time they had finished, when Bron leaned out through the open end of the tent and whistled for Curly and

Moe. The two boars arrived at full charge and left grooves in the dirt as they skidded to a halt next to him.

"Good boys," he said, scratching their bristly skulls. They grunted happily and rolled their eyes up at him. "They think I'm their mother, you know." He waited placidly while Haydin fought with his expression, his face turning red in the process. "That may sound a little funny, but it's true. They were removed from their litter at birth and I raised them. So I'm 'imprinted' as their parent. This is the only way I can be absolutely safe around them, since intelligent as they are, they are still quick-tempered and deadly beasts. It also means that I'm safe as long as they are around. If anyone so much as threatened me, he would be disemboweled within the second. I'm telling you this so you won't try anything foolish. Now, would you kindly hand over that gun you promised not to bring?"

Haydin's hand jumped towards his hip pocket, and stopped just as suddenly as both boars turned towards the sudden movement. Moe was salivating with happiness at the head-scratching and a drop of saliva collected and dropped from the tip of one ten-inch tusk.

"I need it for my own protection . . ." Haydin protested.

"You're better protected without it. Take it out, slowly."

Haydin reached back gingerly and took out a compact energy pistol, then tossed it over to Bron. Bron caught it and hung it on the hook next to the light. "Now empty your pockets," he said. "I want everything metallic dumped onto the box."

"What are you getting at?"

"We'll talk about it later, we don't have time now. Dump."

Haydin looked at the boars and emptied out his pockets, while Bron did the same. They left a collection of coins, keys, knives and small instruments on the box.

"We can't do anything now about the eyelets in your boots," Bron said, "but I don't think that they'll cause much trouble. I took the precaution of wearing elastic-sided boots."

It was dark now and Bron drove his charges into the woods nearby, spreading them out under the trees a good hundred yards from the clearing. Only Queeny, the intelligent sow, remained behind, dropping down heavily next to Bron's stool.

"I demand an explanation," said Governor Haydin.

"Don't embarrass me, Guv, I'm just working on guesses so far. If nothing has happened by morning, I'll give you an explanation—and my apology. Isn't she a beauty?" he added, nodding towards the massive hog at his feet.

"I'm afraid I might use another adjective myself."

"Well don't say it out loud. Queeny's English is pretty good and I don't want her feelings hurt. Misunderstanding, that's all it is. People call pigs dirty, but that's only because they have been made to live in filth. They're naturally quite clean and fastidious animals. They can be fat, they have a tendency to be sedentary and obese—just like people—so they can put on weight if they have the diet for it. In fact they are more like human beings than any other animal. They get ulcers like us and heart trouble the same way we do. Like man, they have hardly any hair on their bodies and even their teeth are similar to ours—their temperaments, too. Centuries ago an early physiologist by the name of Pavlov, who used to experiment with dogs, tried to do the same thing with pigs. But as soon as he placed them on the operating table they would squeal at the top of their lungs and thrash about. He said they were 'inherently hysterical' and went back to working with dogs. Which shows you even the best men have a blind spot. The pigs weren't hysterical—they were plain sensible—it was the dogs who were being dim. The pigs reacted just the way a man might if they tried to tie him down for some quick vivisection . . . What is it, Queeny?"

Bron added this last as Queeny suddenly raised her head, her ears extended, and grunted.

"Do you hear something?" Bron asked. The pig grunted again, a rising tone, and climbed to her feet. "Does it sound like engines coming this way?" Queeny nodded her ponderous head in a very human *yes*.

"Get into the woods, back under the trees!" Bron shouted, hauling Haydin to his feet. "Do it fast—or you're dead."

They ran, headlong, and were among the trees when a distant, rising whine could be heard. Haydin started to ask something but was pushed face first into the leaves as a whining, roaring shape floated into the clearing, occulted blackly against the stars. It was anything but ghostly—but what was it? A swirl of leaves and debris swept over them and Haydin felt something pulling at his legs so that they jumped about of their own accord. He tried to ask a question but his words were drowned out as Bron blew on a plastic whistle and shouted:

"Curly, Moe—*attack!*"

He pulled a stick-like object out of his pack at the same moment and threw it out into the clearing. It hit, popped, and burst into eye-searing flame, a flare of some kind.

The dark shape was a machine, that was obvious enough, round, black and noisy, at least ten feet across, floating a foot above the ground, with a number of circular disks mounted around its edge. One of them swung towards the tent and there was a series of explosive, popping sounds as the tent seemed to explode and fall to the ground.

There was only a moment to see this before the attacking forms of the boars appeared from the opposite side of the clearing. Their speed was incredible as, heads down and legs churning, they dove at the machine. One of them arrived a fraction of a second before the other and crashed into the machine's flank. There was a metallic clang and the shriek of tortured machinery as it was jarred back, bent, almost tipped over.

The boar on the far side took instant advantage of this, his intelligence as quick as his reflexes, and without slowing hurled himself into the air and over the side and into the open top of the machine. Haydin looked on appalled as the first boar did the same thing, the machine was almost on the ground now due either to ruined machinery or the animal's weight, climbing the side and vanishing into the interior. Above the roar of the engine could be heard crashes and metallic tearing—and high-pitched screaming. Something clattered and tore and the sound of the engines died away with a descending moan. As the sound lessened a second machine could be heard approaching.

"Another coming!" Bron shouted, blasting on his whistle as he jumped to his feet. One of the boars popped its head up from the ruins of the machine, then leaped out. The other was still noisily at work. The first boar catapulted himself towards the approaching sound and was on the spot when the machine appeared at the edge of the clearing, leaping and attacking, twisting his tusks into the thing. Something tore and a great black length of material hung down. The machine lurched and the operator must have seen the ruin of the first one, because it skidded in a tight circle and vanished back in the direction from which it had come.

Bron lit a second flare and tossed it out as the first one flickered. They were two-minute flares and the entire action—from beginning to end—had happened in less than that time. He walked over to the ruined machine and Haydin hurried after him. The boar leaped to the ground and stood there panting, then wiped its tusks on the ground.

"What is it?" Haydin asked.

"A hovercraft," Bron said. "They aren't seen very much these days—but they do have their uses. They can move over any kind of open country or water, and they don't leave tracks. But they can't go over or through forest."

"You knew this thing was coming—that's why you had us hide in the woods?"

"I suspected this. And I suspected them." He pointed inside the wrecked hovercraft and Haydin recoiled in shock.

"Blood, green blood, and they're dead. Gray skin, pipe-stem limbs. I've never seen any, just pictures, but could they be . . ."

"Sulbani. You're right. The evidence seemed to point to them, but I couldn't be sure. The use of frequency weapons is typical of them." He kicked at one of the bent disks, not unlike a microwave aerial. "That was the first clue. They have supersonic projectors in the forest, broadcasting on a wavelength that is inaudible but causes a feeling of tension and uneasiness in most animals. That was the ghostly aura that kept people away from this plateau most of the time." He whistled a signal for the herd to assemble. "Animals, as well as men, will move away from the source, and they used it to chase some of the nastier wildlife towards us. When it didn't work and we came back, they sent in the more powerful stuff. Look at your shoes—and at this lantern."

Haydin gasped. The eyelets had vanished from his boots and ragged pieces of lace hung from the torn openings. The lantern, like the metal equipment of the lost expedition, was squeezed and bent out of shape.

"Magnostriction," Bron said. "They were projecting a contracting and expanding magnetic field of an incredible number of gauss. These fields are used to shape metal in factories and the technique works just as well in the field. That, and these projectors to finish the job. They're sonic or microwave. Even a normal scan radar will give you a burn if you stand too close to it, and some supersonic wavelengths can turn water to vapor and explode organic material. That's what they did to your people who camped here. Swept in suddenly, caught them in the tents surrounded by their own equipment, which exploded and crunched and helped to wipe them out. Now let's get going."

"I don't understand what this means, I . . ."

"Later. We have to catch the one that got away."

On the side of the clearing, where the machine had disappeared, a ragged length of black plastic was discovered. "Part of the skirt from the hovercraft," Bron said. "Confines the air and gives more lift. We'll follow them with this." He held out the fabric to Queeny and Jasmine, and the other pigs that pressed up. "As you know dogs track by odor that hangs in the air, and pigs have just as good or better noses. In fact hunting pigs were used in England for years, and pigs are also trained to smell out truffles. There they go!"

Grunting and squealing the pack started away into the darkness and the two men stumbled after them. Haydin had to stop after a few yards and bind his shoes together with strips from his handkerchief before he could go on. He held Bron's belt and Bron had his fingers hooked into the thick bristles that formed a crest on Curly's spine, and they pushed through the forest like this. The hovercraft had to go through open country or their nightmare run would have been impossible.

When a darker mass of mountains loomed ahead Bron

whistled the herd to him. "Stay," he ordered. "Stay with Queeny. Curly, Moe and Jasmine—with me."

They went more slowly now until the grasslands died away in a broken scree of rock at the foot of a nearly vertical cliff. To their left they could make out the black gorge of the river and hear it rushing by below.

"You told me those things can't fly," Haydin said.

"They can't. Jasmine, follow the trail."

The little pig, head up and sniffing, trotted steadily across the broken rock and pointed to the bare side of the cliff.

"Could there possibly be a concealed entrance here?" Haydin asked, feeling the rough texture of the rock.

"There certainly could be—and we have no time to go looking for the key. Get behind those rocks, way over there, while I open this thing up."

He took blocks of a claylike substance from his pack and placed them against the rock, where they remained, over the spot that Jasmine had indicated. Then he pushed a fuse into the explosive, pulled the igniter—and ran. He had just thrown himself down with the others when flame ripped the sky and the ground heaved under them: a spatter of rocks fell on all sides.

They ran forward through the dust and saw light spilling out through a tall crevice in the rock. The boars threw themselves against it and it widened. Once through they saw that a metal door was fastened to a section of rock and could swing outwards to give access to the tunnel they were standing in.

"Attack," Bron said, pointing down the tunnel. "Kill animal things with weapons, try not to kill all."

The boars were gone and the men ran after them. By the time they arrived the battle was over. The Sulbani were knocked out and the complex controls they were working at destroyed for the most part. There were two survivors, and under the watchful eyes of the boars they opened the metal door to a cell.

"I never thought anyone would come," Lea Davies said as she stepped out, half supported by a tall man with the same coloring and eyes.

"Huw Davies?" Bron asked.

"Yes, he is," Haydin said. "But what is happening here? What is this all about?"

"A mine," Huw said, pointing towards a door in the far wall of the room. "A uranium mine—all in secret, and it has been running for years. I don't know how they're getting the metal out, but they mine and partially refine it here, all automatic machinery, and powder the slag and dump it into the river out there."

"I'll tell you what happens then," Bron said. "When they have a cargo it's lifted off by spacer. The Sulbani have very big ideas about moving out of their area and controlling a bigger portion of space. But they are short of power metals and Earth has been keeping it that way. One of the reasons this planet was settled was that it is near the Sulbani sector and, while we didn't need the uranium, we didn't want it falling into the Sulbanis' hands. The Patrol had no idea that they were getting their uranium from Trowbri—though they knew it was coming from someplace—but it was a possibility. When the governor here sent in his request for aid it became an even stronger possibility."

"I still don't understand it," Haydin said. "We would have detected any ships coming to the planet, our radar functions well."

"I'm sure it functions fine—but these creatures have at least one human accomplice who sees to it that the landings are concealed."

"Human . . . !" Haydin gasped, then knotted his fists at the thought. "It's not possible. A traitor to the human race. Who could it be?"

"That's obvious," Bron said, "now that you have been eliminated as a possibility."

"*Me!*"

"You were a good suspect, in the perfect position to cover things up, that's why I was less than frank with you. But you knew nothing about the hovercraft raid and would have been killed if I hadn't pulled you down, so that took you off the list of suspects. Leaving the obvious man, Reymon the radio operator."

"That's right," Lea said. "He let me talk to Huw on the phone, then made me call you or he would have Huw killed. He didn't say why, I didn't know . . ."

"You couldn't have." Bron smiled at her. "He isn't much of a killer and must have been following the Sulbani instructions to get rid of me. He really earned his money by not seeing their ships on radar. And by making sure that the radio communication with Huw's party was cut off when the Sulbani attacked. He probably recorded the signals and gave the murderers an hour or two to do their work before he broadcast the radios' cutting off. That would have helped the mystery."

"Reymon," Governor Haydin said, clenching and unclenching his hands as he looked down at the boars. "Your pigs have had all the fun up to now, and I give them full credit. But let me take care of Reymon myself, without their help."

"You'll have my help," Huw said grimly. "It's my job as well."

"I'll need him as a witness," Bron said.

"He'll be alive," Haydin assured him. "And I can guarantee not only a witness but a complete confession. This settlement has a score to settle with Mr. Reymon."

"Agreed. And I hope you'll give a favorable report about this P.I.G. operation, Governor."

"The absolute best," Haydin said, and looked down at Jasmine who was curled up at his feet chewing on a bar of Sulbani rations. "In fact, I'm almost ready to swear off eating pork for the rest of my life."

FLIGHT OVER XP-637
by Craig Sayre

*Horace Miner once wrote an article called
"Body Ritual Among the Nacirema," which
was a tongue-in-cheek description of the
peculiar habits of Americans as they might
be seen by a visiting anthropologist. The following story contains a similar theme, but
here we have alien scientists studying some
of earth's fabulous creatures.*

Aainst Uthorita paced ruminatively about his behavioral observation laboratory on board the star vessel *Orrespone*, now in a
deep circular orbit about exploratory planet 637. Uthorita was a
scientist, considered one of the best planetary theorists and researchers of extraterrestrial behavior on Giate. He had pio-
neered the concept of studying alien creatures by molecular
trans-alteration, a process by which the molecules of one's body
could be altered and rearranged such that one could assimi-
late the physical appearance and characteristics of an alien creature. Uthorita believed that the best way to study the behavior
of a new alien species was to become one of them and live as
they did.

The aging reptilian paused in front of the battery of electronic equipment that monitored the physiological functions of
his research assistants on the planet below.

When first used, Uthorita's theories and experiments had
proved stunningly successful, yielding a wealth of new information on strange and exotic creatures throughout the star system.
But in recent years, there had been a rising chorus of opposition
to his methods, particularly when they were applied to the
study of creatures living in a violent environment.

The recent events on XP-637 would surely strengthen the

hand of Uthorita's opponents. So much had gone wrong with this project. And now, Uthorita had just received word that one of his ablest assistants had almost been killed while investigating a species of creature on the planet.

Uthorita slowly continued his walk, tugging at the lapels of his open white lab coat while contemplating the consequences of this latest adversity.

It mattered little to him that the Chancellor of Science could demand his resignation. Uthorita was primarily preoccupied with the fate of the injured Saff Enever. And beneath his concern for Enever was an underlying fear of failure. He and his associates had put so much work into this project, and so far they had obtained a considerable quantity of invaluable data on many of the creatures on XP-637. But all that would be lost in the clamor for his dismissal, that incessantly rankled his scales.

Awakened from his thoughts by the gentle sigh of the laboratory door opening, Uthorita stopped pacing and watched his adjutant step briskly into the sterile room.

"Where have you been?" Uthorita snapped in a crusty voice. "Never mind, never mind," he continued before Oistur Rotect could answer the question. "How is Enever?"

Rotect perused the withered saurian features of his mentor; the large, oval, protruding eyes that struggled to remain alert, the hesitating nostrils that fought to draw an even breath, the flinching corners of the mouth that never smiled—all told of the months of excruciating work in space without relief. Rotect knew Uthorita was too old for this type of project now. This would be Uthorita's last mission into deep space. And Rotect, like everyone else on board, had steadfastly remained loyal to Uthorita and wanted this final project to end in success.

"The medicals think they can return him to his own form now. An hour ago, they weren't so sure. Enever is in the molecular recombination chamber at present." Rotect paused, then added, "If all goes well, he will have his own body by the end of the day. After that, no one knows what will happen."

"Well, if he is to die, at least he will die as himself, and not some sordid alien," Uthorita speculated sadly. "I should never have let the two of you talk me into such a dangerous course. I should not have allowed Enever to be transformed into that creature."

"We needed the data to complete the project," Rotect defended the move, and Uthorita knew he was right. "We have to collect data in whatever manner possible. You know better than I, the recombination chamber can only do so much," Rotect commented while jamming one of his gnarled fists into his lab coat.

When Uthorita failed to respond, Rotect continued, "Of the thousands of creatures on XP-637, the chamber can transform us only into those that are approximately the same size as we are. That limits us greatly in our research. Enever and I believed that it was a reasonable risk, in view of the fact that no one had ever been transformed into that species before " Rotect bowed his wrinkled head. "I guess we were wrong."

"No," Uthorita replied. "I am to blame for any failure. I should have known better. I should have assigned Enever another creature, one that leads a less violent life."

"That would have been very difficult," Rotect stated. "On XP-637 life feeds on violence and death."

"Perhaps you're right," Uthorita agreed, then pondered aloud, "A most baffling planet, this XP-637. It is the first one we've encountered where the mammals, who were the last to arrive, are the highest order of life, while the reptiles are one of the lowest. Even the birds are more evolved. On all the other planets we've encountered, where mammals, birds and reptiles coexist, the reptiles evolved before the mammals and birds, and consequently advanced the furthest. Do you suppose that could be an explanation for all the violence on XP-637?"

"That is a possibility," Rotect replied. "That's one of the items we're trying to determine."

Of the 637 exploratory planets studied, Rotect had personally explored fifteen and participated in the exploration of another twenty. He knew that Uthorita had headed planetary projects of at least twice that many.

"It's tragic, but we may never find out," Uthorita sighed. "We have over a hundred transformed researchers on the planet's surface now, and this latest incident may condemn the entire project."

Uthorita subconsciously began rubbing the virescent scales on his forehead, and Rotect automatically glanced at the five shriveled fingers on Uthorita's hand. The sixth had been lost in a recombination chamber malfunction years ago.

"I stopped by Communications on my way here," Rotect stated.

"And?" Uthorita flared, startling Rotect.

"A complete report of the incident has been sent to the Chancellor of Science," Rotect continued.

Uthorita hissed in exasperation. "Then indeed, it is the end of the project." He slammed his good hand on a cluttered countertop.

Rotect jumped at the unexpected crack, and almost dropped the folder he'd been carrying. "Not necessarily. The Chancellor must review all the facts."

He tried to sound as optimistic as possible, but his statement failed to offer any encouragement to Uthorita.

Rotect tried again. "He may just redirect the project." Uthorita's somber expression remained intact. "The communicators gave me the transcript of Enever's last transmission."

That recaptured Uthorita's attention. "I didn't think they could make any sense out of it."

"They were finally able to computer-enhance the recording several times. It's still garbled in places, and the beginning was beyond retrieval, but you can still get a feeling for what happened."

Rotect opened the folder and handed its contents to Uthorita.

Uthorita glanced at the first page, then at Rotect. "What do all those creatures down there call XP-637?"

"Earth," Rotect answered.

"Earth," Uthorita repeated. The word seemed to stick in his throat. "That's a very odd name, but then, there are many odd creatures there." He returned to the first page and began to read:

. . . (Incoherent) . . . and flying in three parallel V-formations at . . . (unintelligible) . . . altitude. There were thirty-eight others in the flight, besides myself. I was between Formation Leader

Stanley and Wing Guide 2nd Class Wignan in C-group. Flight Commander Montgomery was leading all three formations. Except for routine navigational instructions, no one had broken silence since we took off.

Within an hour of our departure, the first soft pink rays of dawn were emanating from the southeast horizon, lending some definition to the achromatic landscape below. High overhead, the scattered puffs of cumulus clouds gave stark contrast to the emerging sapphire sky. The weather appeared to be holding and we had a slight tail wind.

Far below, two sweeping highways merged into one at a congested junction. Most of the creeping vehicles had extinguished their lights by now. We made a slight course correction in order to fly parallel to the highway that ran north. We continued to follow it until it angled to the northeast.

As the sun began its journey across the early spring sky, the serene countryside took on the form of velvet marshes stretching in all directions, broken only by an irregular pattern of small farms connected by narrow, unpaved roads.

Montgomery motioned for us to veer a little more to the west. Blue Flight lost four birds yesterday while flying over that clump of mangled trees just ahead. All three formations banked into a gentle turn to the left, then straightened again. Everyone stared at the serried undergrowth far to our right to see if there would be any response to our maneuver. But all was quiet.

Ahead of us, I could see over three dozen distinct objects spread out in a line, traveling at our course, speed and altitude. We were now following Red Flight, which was about a mile in front of us.

Our anxiety rose as we approached the shallow stream ahead, the southern boundary of Demon's Strip. Everyone felt the tension, the fear, as we began our flight over the hundred mile wide stretch of bogs and marshes, over which there have been more losses than any other comparable portion of land. We instinctively began to go a little faster, push a little harder. We were more alert, scanning the swampy terrain below for the slightest hint of trouble.

The strain was particularly telling on those who had made

these flights many times before. These hardened veterans knew what could be expected. They had repeatedly lived through the horrors of seeing their fellow comrades blasted from the skies. One notable old flier, Wing Protect 1st Class Curtis, was making his last flight. He had amassed many stories of courage and heroism which he would tell over and over to the younger fliers during the long winter nights when no one could fly. Much of what I have previously reported has come from Curtis' recollections. He longed to spend his final days in peace and solitude.

The younger, greener fliers, though still afraid, relished the thrill and excitement of risking their lives to reach their home waters. Several had stood around before takeoff, boasting of their abilities to outmaneuver anything that was thrown up against them. I myself, having never made the flight before, tended to be very apprehensive about it all, and I had no intention of proving how brave I was.

Suddenly, the silence was broken. "Did you see it?" Wing Guide 3rd Class Gilman called out. "Low, and just ahead, next to that small patch of water." He waited for someone to verify his sighting, then said, "A flash, or reflection, right where the sun hits the shoreline."

Everyone strained to catch a glimpse of the light. Binoculars? Perhaps a gunsight? Or was it merely a tossed aside beer can?

Montgomery wasn't taking any chances, even though Red Flight had passed uneventfully over the pond. He knew it was a common tactic to allow the first flight to pass unscathed, then ambush the following one. He began to lead the group in a wide arc to the left, while dispatching Wing Protect 3rd Class Longly to fly reconnaissance over the area. Longly quickly rolled out of formation and dove towards the shallow water. He buzzed the shoreline several times at high speed while the flight continued its detour, then climbed hard and fast to rejoin his formation. He hadn't seen anything unusual.

By the time we were back on course, Red Flight was far ahead and just barely visible.

The sun was well on its way towards mid-morning and the subtle hues of the dawn light were now sharply contrasting shades of green and brown. The sky above was a solid, brilliant blue, interrupted occasionally by the high, white puffy clouds.

Then, without warning, several flashes of light twinkled directly below Red Flight. Almost immediately, two of their fliers tumbled wildly out of control, then plummeted to earth. We watched helplessly as another was hit. That one tried to keep up but, exhausted and mortally wounded, he soon began to descend.

Montgomery gave the order to climb and turn west. Another detour. I looked towards Red Flight as we headed for our new course. They were taking a terrible pounding. By now, they had lost almost half their flight, yet they still held their formation and pressed on through the withering fire.

Each among us must have shared the same thought. Would it be our turn next?

But we flew on without interruption. However, we had lost precious time again by avoiding dangerous air space, and there was little we could do to make it up.

"Flak ahead!" Flight Leader Stanley shouted.

I could see nothing in the sky, but there were the telltale flashes on the ground. They seemed to be everywhere, sending up a barrage of shot. But what were they firing at?

Montgomery hesitated. Should he order another detour, or risk flying through? Finally, he dipped his wings, the signal for the group to turn.

But as we straightened out on our new heading, the entire area below erupted with the deadly orange flashes.

"I'm hit!" cried Flight Leader Byron as he dropped back from A-group. He struggled to remain with us, but it was hopeless.

"Commander, help me!" screamed someone else. It was Wing Guide 3rd Class Dickinson. His entire left wing had been shot away. He spun crazily earthward and crashed into a shallow pool of stagnant water.

"Come on! Keep up! Keep going!" Montgomery shouted encouragement to everyone.

We could hear the hideous pounding of the dreaded guns below, while straining for every ounce of speed we could muster. The eerie snaps of the projectiles breaking the sound barrier were all around us, and the air was filled with a foul, acid smell.

"Get back in formation!" Montgomery yelled to a couple of green fliers from B-group who had just broken away in panic and were diving wildly for any cover the ground could provide.

Yet both ignored Montgomery's command and continued their descent. Midway down, one took a direct hit, and was blown apart. The other managed to reach the swampy terrain, but was quickly blasted into oblivion.

"Stay at altitude!" Formation Leader Stanley ordered everyone. "Keep up!"

But Curtis could not. He was dropping back further and further.

"You go on," he yelled to everyone. "I'll be all right."

But he wasn't. Within seconds he was struck twice. He coughed and slowed, struggling to keep his nose up, then rolled and deliberately dove right at one of the gun positions. For an instant, it seemed as though every weapon was trained on old Curtis. He let out a terrible raging shriek just before all the guns fired simultaneously. It was doubtful that any part of him ever hit the ground.

He did not die in vain, though. He bought us the precious seconds we needed to reach a small, low hanging cloud for cover. When the flight emerged from the other side, the air was silent and peaceful again, as though nothing had happened.

For the remainder of the day, we flew on unmolested. No one would talk about what had happened, but we all knew we had been extremely fortunate. The flight had lost only five birds, which was a remarkable achievement for the Demon's Strip run at this time of year.

I wondered what had become of Red Flight, which I hadn't seen since we took evasive action when they came under fire. Had any of them made it at all?

. . . (pause in transmission) . . .

It is late afternoon now and our landing site looms on the horizon ahead. There will be much jubilation when we reach our destination, so I have compiled the events of today during the previous hour and transmitted them to you, rather than wait until I've landed. Celebrations after a flight such as this one are in the grand tradition and I may be unable to send any more data for a few days. I have tried to be as thorough as possible in the allotted time, and I will answer all questions at a debriefing when I return. I will, however, transmit the landing proceedings as they occur.

. . . (pause in transmission) . . .

We are circling over the site now, and there are several who have already landed. They must be the remainder of Red Flight. They appear to be very quiet though.

Montgomery motions for A-group to begin their approach. One by one, they break away from their V-formation, roll and begin their descent.

. . . (pause in transmission) . . .

The first ones are touching down when Montgomery signals B-group to follow.

. . . (pause in transmission) . . .

Finally it is our turn. I am watching two fliers on my right roll out. Now I am rolling and heading for earth. It's so beautiful up here, I really . . . (incoherent) . . .

. . . (too much static) . . . Two fliers from A-group are scrambling to take off again. That seems very strange. I am at less than a thousand feet now and I can't locate anyone nearby to find out what is happening.

Perhaps I could—no wait! They're yelling something. "Decoy, decoy!" I think that's what they're saying.

Now everyone is trying to take off. Oh my . . . (sounds of gunfire and explosions) . . . It's an ambush! We're under attack from all sides! . . . (more gunfire, cries for help in the background) . . .

. . . (incoherent) . . . desperately trying to get airborne, but they're being shot down almost before they lift off. It's horrible! . . . (unintelligible) . . . a massacre!

Those in C-group that are still flying have aborted their landing approach and are scattering in all directions . . . I'm starting to climb and turn south . . . smoke everywhere.

No! Montgomery is going down!

I've got to . . . (impact sound, static, Enever has been injured) . . . I'm hit! I . . . I can't move! I'm falling! . . . I'm going in! Rotect, help me! Rotect! . . . (impact).

Uthorita sighed as he slapped the stack of pages down on the counter. What a foolish thing to let Enever do, he thought. "Did you have much trouble getting him back?"

"When his emergency finder signal stopped, we immediately instigated a search. He wasn't hard to locate," Rotect answered. "But we had to wait until dark before we could recover him. At least those dogs didn't get him though."

Both scientists turned as a medical entered the lab. "I thought you'd want to know," he said, then smiled. "Enever is out of danger. He's going to be all right."

A wave of relief overcame the old researcher. "Thank you," Uthorita said in a low, raspy voice.

"It will be some time before he can return to his work, though," the medic said.

"Perhaps all of us could use a rest," Uthorita responded.

The medic started to leave, then paused. "Oh, I almost forgot. A communicator gave me this to pass along to you."

He handed the message to Uthorita, then departed. Rotect could see the top priority seal on the outside.

Uthorita suddenly looked bleak again. "It's from the Chancellor of Science," he muttered as he slowly opened the envelope.

But as his tired eyes scanned the contents, his expression lightened considerably.

"Well? Well?" Rotect asked excitedly.

"It seems as though the Chancellor isn't too pleased with some of our techniques and decisions," Uthorita paraphrased, "but he is giving us ten more days to complete the project."

"I'm sure we can be finished by then," Rotect said enthusiastically.

"Yes, I believe you're right," Uthorita answered musingly, and Rotect detected just a hint of a saurian smile. "You know, it's really a pity we couldn't become the hunter instead of the hunted."

"Sir?" Rotect asked, having no idea what Uthorita was talking about.

"Think of it, Rotect," Uthorita was already mapping his next project. "We have only one side of a classical confrontation that takes place all the time on XP-637, that of the hunted. Suppose we could see it from the other side, the hunter's point of view. What a thesis that would be."

"You know that's impossible," Rotect said. "None of us could ever be transformed into a human. They're much too large. Why, we had enough trouble transforming Enever into a migrant duck."

"Well, like I said, it's just a pity, that's all," Uthorita said. "Strange creatures, those humans. Someday, though, we'll devise a way to actively study their behavior too."

"Someday," Rotect echoed.

THE BEES FROM BORNEO
by Will H. Gray

*Newspapers love to write about the so-called
killer bees. However, the critters they refer
to are mere pussycats when compared with
the creations of mad scientist Silas Donaghy.
Indeed, moral issues raised by the ability to
manipulate genes threaten to become some
of the thorniest science has ever had to face.*

Silas Donaghy was by far the best beekeeper and queen breeder
in the United States; not because of the amount of honey he
produced but because he had bred a strain of bees that produced records. Those two hundred hives consistently averaged
three hundred pounds of honey each. Naturally enough, everyone who had read about his results in the different bee journals
wanted queens from his yard, and his yearly production of two
thousand queens was always bought up ahead of time at two
dollars each, which is just double the usual price.

Silas was a keen student of biology besides an expert beekeeper. He had tried all the usual experiments with different
races of bees before falling back on Italian stock, bred for many
generations in the United States for honeygathering qualities,
gentleness, and color.

Although he had achieved commercial success, he still
found the experimental side most fascinating, especially with
regard to artificial fertilization of drone eggs—a comparatively
simple matter, only requiring a little care. His greatest ambition
was to cross-breed different species and even different genera.
From his studies he found out that the freaks exhibited in side
shows were not crosses between dog and rabbit or cat and dog,
as advertised, such things being impossible, owing, it is thought,
to chemical differences in the life germs.

Every beekeeper knows that the queen bee lays fertile or unfertile eggs at will. One mating is sufficient for life, and after it the queen can lay a million or more fertile eggs at the rate of as many as two thousand a day in summer. The fertile eggs become females, either workers or queens, depending on how they are fed, while the unfertile eggs hatch out into drones, which are the big, clumsy, stingless males. For the most part they are useless, for they require the labor of five workers to keep them fed, and only a very few ever perform the services for which they were created. Nature is very bounteous when it comes to reproduction, but seems to desert her children once they are safely ushered into this wicked world.

All might have gone well if someone had not sent Silas Donaghy a queen bee from the wilds of Borneo. After careful examination, he introduced it to one of his hives which he had just deprived of its own queen. In a month's time the new brood had hatched and were on the wing; pretty bees they were with a red tuft on the abdomen and long, graceful bodies with strong wings. Soon the honey began to come in and pile up on that hive, which was mounted on a weighing scale. Up and up crept the weight until Silas saw that he had something as far beyond his own strain as his own were above the ordinary black bee. In his enthusiasm for these new and beautiful creatures, he overlooked the source of their honey. Not alone did they gather from the flowers but from every plant that had sweet juice in its stems or leaves, and they did not hesitate to enter other hives and rob them of their stores. In fact, wherever there was a sign of sugar, they seemed to find it and carry it off. When that hive had piled up a thousand pounds of honey, Silas took eggs from it and put them in every hive he had. Risking everything, he bought extra hives and equipment and raised five thousand of the new queens, which he sold for five dollars each. Soon his mail was flooded with letters of two kinds: one lot praising his queens as the most wonderful honey gatherers in the world, the other abusing him for scattering a race of robbers that were ruining crops and cleaning out all other hives within a radius of five miles.

Things might have righted themselves if it had not been for a California senator who owned two thousand hives and had them completely robbed out by another beekeeper who had only five hundred, all mothered by the new Borneo strain.

By means of influence at Washington, and without consulting the Bureau of Entomology, this senator had the mails closed to Silas Donaghy's queens. It was a dreadful shock to Silas because he had already begun refunding people their money and replacing the queens free of charge. Now he could no longer make amends, but the letters of abuse continued to come in by the hundred. He said nothing, but devoted himself more and more to his experiments.

It was with an ordinary wasp or yellow jacket that he succeeded in producing a creature that soon turned the continent upside down.

Under his super-microscope he was looking at an unfertile egg of a Borneo queen. Something buzzed into the room and flew around the microscope, making a breeze that threatened to blow away the delicate egg from its glass slide. Impatiently he put out his hand and to his surprise caught something between his fingers. It was a drone wasp and he had partly crushed it. An idea suddenly struck him; he took a fine camel's-hair brush and touched it to the fluid containing the microscopic spermatazoa or life germs exuding from the dead wasp. With infinite care he applied the brush to the large end of the tiny, cucumber-shaped egg on the stage of the microscope. Presently he saw several minute, eel-like creatures burrowing into the egg. One outswam the others; its long tail was replaced by protoplasmic radiations and it united with the female pronucleus. With a tense look, the experimenter sat on with his eye rigidly glued to the microscope.

Had he succeeded? Would cleavage take place? He was called to lunch, but the call went unheeded. At last the pronucleus elongated, became narrow in the middle and finally split into two.

Wonderful! Extraordinary! It would seem that he had accomplished that which no other man had ever done.

Carefully he transferred the wonderful egg to a queen cup and covered it with royal jelly, that special food that in quantity would make it a queen.

Now he must trust it to the tender mercies of the bees,

for no man knows the exact constituents of the food fed to the larvae day by day. Then there is always the chance that the bees will reject the egg thus offered to them; they show their disapproval by licking up the royal jelly and devouring the delicate egg.

Silas went through agonies in those three days that it takes the egg to hatch. Everything went as it should, and in fourteen days he had a perfect queen resembling a wasp except for a few reddish hairs on the abdomen. His anxieties were not yet over, for a week after hatching the queen goes on her wedding flight. High up into the air she soars with all the drones after her in a flock. To the strong goes the victory, but his joy is short lived, for after one embrace he falls to the ground, dead, his vitals torn from him and attached to the queen. Such is the queen's first flight and after it she returns to the hive to lay countless thousands of eggs. Had he wished to, Silas could have fertilized the queen by the Sladen method, almost amounting to an operation, but he thought it wiser to let nature take her course.

On the seventh day the young queen came out of the hive, ran about the alighting board nervously for a minute, then took a short flight to get her bearings and finally shot into the air and out of sight while the drones followed in desperate haste.

Silas waited and watched, but she did not return. Days passed and his spirits fell to zero, for the chance of a lifetime had slipped from his grasp.

It was a month or so later that young Silas came running into his father's study one morning with the news:

"Oh, Father! Come quick and bring the cyanide. There's a wasp's nest bigger than a pumpkin down on a tree in the wood lot."

"Now, Silas, I've often told you not to exaggerate. You know it isn't that size."

"Well, Father, it's enormous, anyway."

When Silas, senior, went down to investigate he found his son's description not in the least exaggerated. If anything, the size was underestimated. There, to his astonishment, hung the largest wasp's nest he had ever seen or heard about. The insects going in and out seemed different from the ordinary yellow jackets. Walking over to investigate, he received a sting that temporarily knocked him out. He was well inoculated to bee stings and they hardly affected him, but this was something quite different. Some way or other he reached the house and collapsed on the doorstep.

It was three days before he was about again, feeling very shaky on his legs. He did not lack courage, for he took a butterfly net and veil and went down to see how the new insects were getting along. The nest was bigger still and the numbers of bees coming in and out had greatly increased. He managed to capture one before he was chased home, and a sting on the hand, though very painful, did not incapacitate him so badly as the first had done.

To his astonishment the captured insect had the red tip to its abdomen. Here was a great discovery. His escaped queen had settled down on her own account and started a paper-pulp nest like ordinary wasps instead of returning to her own hive. Interest in the new species overcame everything else in his mind, even the severity of the sting.

Putting the captured specimen in a queen mailing cage, he posted it to the professor of entomology at the State University, who had been friendly to him through all his late troubles. Alas for the regulations which he had quite forgotten in his excitement. The Post Office people returned his specimen with a prosecution notice. He was summoned to court and heavily fined.

While he was away from home, little Silas was stung by one of the bees and died the same evening.

Something gave way in the poor man's mind and he hated the whole world with a deadly hatred.

Making himself a perfectly bee-tight costume, he sat near the great nest for hours at a time, capturing young queens as they emerged. Next he bought a gross of little rubber balloons and some cylinders of compressed hydrogen. Making small paper cages, he attached an inflated balloon to each, put in a young queen and started them off wherever the wind would take them. When the queen got tired of her paper prison, she chewed her way out to freedom and, single-handed, started a new colony.

It was getting late in the season and the new strain of insects did not make much headway before the cold weather set in.

Early the next spring the country papers began to complain of the prevalence of deaths from bee or wasp stings. Every year some people die of stings, but now the number was greatly increased. Animals also were frequently found dead without apparent reason. Many people got stung and recovered after a week in bed.

In the cities these constant accounts from the country became a sort of joke. The words "stung," "sting," and "stings" were used on every occasion, in season and out. When a man was away from work without permission, instead of saying he was burying his grandmother he said he had been laid up with a bee sting.

At last official notice was taken of the new menace and they were recognized as being descended from the famous Borneo queens. The bees from Borneo were now discussed in every state in the Union. The cities were still joking, but the country people were getting desperate. Many had sold out for what they could get and had moved to parts not yet infested with the new pest. Those that remained wore special clothes, had all doors and windows carefully screened, and took every precaution not to let the insects into the house. It was soon discovered that even the chimneys had to be covered when fires were not burning. The new insects had to have sugar as well as insect or flesh diet, but they preferred to get their sweets in any other way rather than from the flowers. All beehives were quickly robbed and the bees killed off. Soon it was realized that there would be no fruit crop in many districts, for even if pickers could be found who would run the risk of being stung, the insects were always ahead of them devouring the fruit as soon as ripe.

The cities began to wake up when the new insects found that open fruit stalls and candy stores were theirs for the taking. They built their nests from waste paper or old wood or any fibrous material that they could find. The nests were built high up under cornices and gables where it was very difficult to find them and still more difficult to destroy them. The death toll was now greater, for the city people were not inoculated as many of the country folk were. One in every four died from the stings. The conversation became more serious, the papers had a special column for deaths from stings. A fellow worker would not turn up at the office; his friends looked at each other gravely and cast lots to see who should ring up to find out the sad news. If he did come back after being in a hospital he was hailed with enthusiasm.

All the leading scientists and doctors were working hard to devise a serum or antitoxin. Some brave men were undergoing a series of injections with formic acid to see if it would immunize them. Every newspaper had a list of so-called cures sent in by people who professed to have cured themselves or others. It was hard to judge these things, for it was impossible to know if the sting were really of a Borneo queen and not of some other hymenopterous insect. Panic alone killed many, so great was the fright of those stung by any insect. Those who recovered from a sting practically never died when stung again; this fact was of great use when recruiting began later on in the year.

A dreadful catastrophe raised the menace of the bees to an importance exceeding everything else.

A trainload of molasses was entering a suburb of a great city where the bees had obtained quite a foothold. The engineer was stung in the face and staggered back into the arms of the fireman. A lurch and both fell out on the track. On rushed the heavy train with throttle open. Soon it entered the yards at great speed, jumped the switches and collided with an outgoing passenger train. Sounds of rending steel and splintering wood filled the air. Roaring, hissing steam drowned the cries of the injured. Over track and wreckage spread a turgid mass of strong-smelling molasses.

Before the work of rescue was half completed the air was swarming with millions of buzzing insects. Doctors, nurses, railway workers, policemen and ambulance drivers were stung into insensibility and death. To complete the awful drama some well-intentioned persons bravely started smudge fires, hoping to smoke away the bees. Now fire was added and the flames licked through the seething, treacly mass, converting it into a holocaust such as had not been witnessed since the days of the Great War. Five hundred persons lost their lives through accident, fire and stings. Thirty or forty casualties, at the most, would have been the total if it had not been for the bees.

The nation was awake now. Complete destruction of this new pest was demanded in all the great newspapers. Expense could not be spared in such an emergency. There must be no half-hearted measures, for the very life of the country was being strangled by the creation of a madman.

Volunteers were organized all over the country. They were equipped with extension ladders and strong sacks, which they put over the suspended nest, drew tight the running string, and transferred the whole thing to a woven wire burner, where it was sprayed with gasoline and burnt. At first they seemed to make some headway, but a fine spell of weather and millions of emerging young queens gave the bees fresh impetus and the newly started nests could not be found so easily as the large old ones.

The national capital proved a specially happy hunting ground for the bees. The public buildings provided thousands of nooks and corners where the nests were not discovered until they were as large as barrels. Sometimes the weight would break them down. If they fell in a street, there were sure to be many deaths before traffic could be diverted, and men protected to the last degree destroyed the insects with flaming sprays and poison gas. At last things became so bad that the seat of government was moved to a town in Arizona which had not yet been invaded by bees.

Many new industries sprang into being, for anything advertised to combat the pests found a ready sale. Traps of every size, shape and description were sold; many of them more ingenious to look at than practical in use. Poison baits were sold and used by the ton, many harmless animals and not a few children fell victims to their use.

In spite of everything the pests went on increasing in numbers until the country seemed on the verge of bankruptcy. When

farm mortgages, considered so safe, fell due, it was not worth-
while foreclosing them, for the land was useless. The new insects did not pollinate the fruit, but they destroyed the insects
that did. Farm produce rose to unheard-of prices. Passenger
traffic was reduced to a minimum, for nobody traveled who
could possibly avoid it. Excursions and pleasure trips seemed
to be a thing of the past. Even free insurance against stings
did not stimulate travel, for no one seemed keen on being stung,
however big the compensation to their heirs!

When fruit reached a certain price, large syndicates bought
up fertile stretches for almost nothing and screened them in at
enormous cost. In these enclosures the most intensive culture
known was practiced with very profitable results. Not alone
were there gardeners, but numerous guards patrolled the high
framework with shotguns charged with salt ready to shoot any
bee that should find its way in. Common bees had to be introduced from great distances for pollination purposes.

Silas Donaghy gibbered and raved in the state asylum; when he
saw anyone stung he was convulsed with mirth. From morning
to night he played tricks on the attendants, doctors and other
patients. They never could tell when he might have a bee concealed about his clothing or wrapped in his handkerchief. It
was most disturbing to the officials to get suddenly chased by a
man who held sudden death in his hand. They put him in the
padded cell, but it did not disturb him in the least. When his
food was brought, he imitated the buzzing of a bee so skillfully
that the attendant dropped the food and ran, followed by Silas'
unearthly shrieks of merriment. At times he appeared quite
sane and would skillfully catch and kill every bee that acci-
dentally got let in. When he got stung himself, which was very
rarely, he would wince with the pain and fall to his knees and
grope about half blinded for support while the poison coursed
through his veins. Getting to his feet again, he would stagger
about with the tears of agony running down his cheeks, the while
laughing at himself and cursing his weakness. Those who saw
him marveled, for most people collapsed in a writhing heap
and mercifully became unconscious.

In his sane moments he begged for his beloved microscope

and experimental equipment. At last, to humor him and incidentally save themselves unlimited trouble, they gave him a little hut in the grounds where he could do as he liked so long as he did not annoy anyone. The first thing he did was to tear off all the screen wire and let the bees have free access to his living and sleeping rooms. He even let them share his meals and they sat in rows on the edge of his plate. It wasn't long before there was a nest right above his bed; it remained there undisturbed, for no one went near his little abode. The official bee swatters kept clear of Silas, for they had their dignity to uphold and Silas made fun of their bee-tight costumes and elaborate equipment. He could kill more bees in a day, if he wanted to, than they could in a week.

The Government was still busy working out methods to control the plague. One that seemed to promise some success was the introduction of a large fly belonging to the hawk-like family that prey on honey bees, catching them on the wing and tearing them asunder to feed on the sweet juices within. These flies were bred in great numbers and distributed over the country. Spiders and bee-eating birds were also extensively tried out.

With the first days of autumn the nation breathed more freely, for the Borneo bees were even more sensitive to cold than the ordinary hive bees. So great was the relief that all the activities of summer began to take place in the winter. People went visiting and the railways ran excursions. Such is the spirit of the people that they quickly forget their troubles and trust that the past will bury its past. But the entomologists of the country knew and trembled at the thought of spring when the fine weather would entice from their wintering places thousands and millions of queens that would quickly construct nests and raise broods that would far exceed anything that had yet gone before. A bounty of ten cents a queen was offered and thousands of people collected the dormant insects from their hiding places. Special instructors visited all the schools, telling of the dangers that awaited them if the queens were not destroyed now.

The fine weather came and with it the queens came out of their hiding places in countless millions. Those gathered were as a drop in the bucket, compared to those left undisturbed.

For a few short weeks things got steadily worse and worse. All the devices of the previous year were used and a lot of new ones. Single screen doors were no longer of any use. Double doors were better, but the most reliable system proved to be a cold passage kept at a very low temperature. In this passage the insects became chilled and could be swept up and destroyed.

Every day now seemed closer to the time when things would end. A heat wave came along and the overstrained public services collapsed. The dead lay in the streets. The frantic telephone calls went unanswered. Even the water pipes were choked with the dead insects and the water tainted with the acrid poison that also filled the air.

Those who had the means and were able fled to other parts where the breakdown had not yet occurred. The military forces of the country were fully organized for relief purposes and those who remained were rescued from the cities of the dead.

The State Lunatic Asylum collapsed with all the rest of society and patients wandered out and were soon stung to death.

Silas was undecided what to do at first. Then he thought it would be a good plan to put the screen wire back on his shack. The bees objected to the hammering, so he waited until night and did it then. He was rather disappointed at having to destroy the nest inside, but it could not be helped. Several visits to the storeroom of the asylum yielded all the food he needed. For a few days he remained in solitude, then he packed his beloved microscope, put on a light bee veil and started home over the deserted roads. He was careful not to annoy the insects in any way. He never batted at them or made quick, jerky movements and he avoided going near their nests. He took it very easy so that he would not perspire, for bees hate the smell of sweat.

Sad sights met his gaze as he trudged along. The whitened bones of cows and horses and smaller animals littered the fields, for the insects picked their victims clean, requiring as they did a partly animal diet like ordinary wasps. A disabled truck stood by the roadside and sitting in the driver's seat was a grim skeleton. Further on a cheap touring car lay on its side and four skeletons, two large and two small, told the sad tale of a family wiped out in a few minutes. These sights did not seem to affect Silas at all; he was more interested in the nests that hung from every tree and telegraph pole and from the gables and eaves of houses and barns. Once he was overtaken by an armored and screened military ambulance. He refused their aid and they hurried on, the wheels crushing a bee at every turn. A crushed bee is smelled by the other bees and they are immediately on the warpath, so Silas had to leave the road and take to the fields.

When he reached home he found his wife alone in the well-screened house. She had been ostracized by all the neighbors long before they had left, and but for Silas' letters of instruction, she could not have carried on single-handed. Somehow she had expected Silas. He entered by the cellar steps and slipped through so dexterously that only seven bees got in with him. They flew to a window, where he quickly killed them, for Mrs. Donaghy, strange to say, had never been stung. He took off his outer-clothing and found five more. Disposing of these, he went upstairs and carried his microscope to the study, where he carefully unpacked it and put a glass cover over it. He fussed about the study in an absent-minded way until Mrs. Donaghy called him to supper. Sitting down, he looked at the place where little Silas used to sit.

"Where's the boy?" he questioned. "You know I like him to be on time to his meals."

A pained look came over the poor lady's face.

"Silas, you know he's gone."

"Gone where? What do you mean?"

She looked up flushing and for the first time in her married life spoke with heat:

"Dead, you know he's dead; stung to death by one of your accursed bees."

Silas collapsed on the table. Covering his face with his hands, great sobs wracked his body. "My God, my God, what have I done?" he moaned.

Presently he was in his study again, looking at everything with a new light in his eyes. He was alert and methodical now, and there was a set appearance about his jaw that had not been there for a long, long while.

Taking the plug out of the keyhole, he waited till a bee came in and dexterously catching it by the wings, brought it to his study. His tired eyes were bright now and he appeared to be looking at something he had never seen before. Frequently he came to the living-room to ask his wife questions about what had happened in the last year or so. He seemed appalled, but a glance from any window verified all she said.

That night he visited a deep bee cellar constructed underground where he used to winter some of his colonies. He found that it had been used as an ice house while he had been away. Seeing an old hive in the corner, he went over and lifted the lid. To his utter astonishment a faint buzz greeted him that was quite different from the high note of the all-pervading pest outside. Here was the remnant of a colony of honey bees that had been forgotten. How could they have survived all this time? He didn't know, unless it was the ice making a continuous winter for two years. Shouldering the hive, he carried it out and placed it in a little screened chicken yard where Mrs. Donaghy had endeavored to raise a few vegetables. Next morning the survivors were buzzing about getting their bearings, though there wasn't much fear of their straying very far in the little enclosure.

For the next week Silas hardly slept or took time to eat. If he wasn't at the microscope he was in the small yard where the last honey bees in North America flew about and licked up the honey given them. Little they knew that the fate of a continent depended on them.

At last he produced a drone that seemed to fill the requirements. It must be able to outfly the drones of the vicious half-breeds all around. It must be able to produce grandsons, for by the laws of parthenogenesis a drone cannot have sons that would also be swift and amorous. It must produce daughters and granddaughters resembling honey bees and incapable of surviving the winter alone.

Most scientists would have waited to test out these qualities before scattering the new product broadcast. Silas, however, was always impetuous, as the sale of his first Borneo queens had shown him to be. He realized now that the situation might be better but could not be worse.

Setting to work in his little enclosure, he bred drones in large numbers and liberated them. If only he had some way of distributing them quickly! Balloons and hydrogen? Alas, he had neither. He wandered about, thinking hard. There in the basement stood the little lighting plant with its neat row of batteries and a large jar of acid in the corner. Ha! There was hydrogen, either by electrolysis or more quickly still with strips of zinc or nails and the acid. Paper bags would do for the balloons.

In a day or so he was sending the drones off on the wind by the dozen together, hoping that they would seek out the young queens wherever they went and father a new race of harmless bees that would die out entirely in the winter.

In a month he noticed young queens without the familiar red tuft on their tails. Capturing a few, he put them in his enclosure and fed them carefully, even opening a precious tin of meat to help them along; but they did not respond and some died. They were incapable of living alone. However, those put into nests flourished and outdid their vicious half-sister. It was a treat to see the new drones on the wing rushing about in their wild search for virgin queens. The workers of the new breed had barbed stings and died on using them. It was not very painful either.

Every day now Silas was in his garden getting things to rights, planting and harvesting. He smiled now at the millions of bees, for they were all different from the old race that was quickly dying off.

He often wondered if there was anyone else alive. Making a trip to the deserted village, he was rummaging around looking for canned goods when he was astonished to hear a telephone ring. It was a long distance call searching for anyone alive.

"The bees have played themselves out," he was told. "The breed did not hold true. Nature righted herself automatically."

Silas went home smiling. He knew that he had started and ended the awful plague.

THE ANGLERS OF ARZ
by Roger Dee

*Like the earlier story by Craig Sayre, this tale
deals with scientific attempts to understand
members of an alien species. But in this case,
the scientists are earth men and the aliens
consist of humanlike land creatures, squidlike
water creatures and gigantic flying reptiles
who all inhabit a bizarre world of tiny islands
surrounded by an ocean with an under-
water city.*

The third night of the *Marco Four's* landfall on the moonless
Altarian planet was a repetition of the two before it, a nine-hour
intermission of drowsy, pastoral peace. Navigator Arthur Farrell
—it was his turn to stand watch—was sitting at an open-side port
with a magnoscanner ready; but in spite of his vigilance he had
not exposed a film when the inevitable pre-dawn rainbow began
to shimmer over the eastern ocean.

Sunrise brought him alert with a jerk, frowning at sight of
two pinkish, bipedal Arzian fishermen posted on the tiny coral
islet a quarter-mile offshore, their blank triangular faces turned
stolidly toward the beach.

"They're at it again," Farrell called, and dropped to the
mossy turf outside. "Roll out on the double! I'm going to
magnofilm this!"

Stryker and Gibson came out of their sleeping cubicles
reluctantly, belting on the loose shorts which all three wore in
the balmy Arzian climate. Stryker blinked and yawned as he
let himself through the port, his fringe of white hair tousled
and his naked paunch sweating. He looked, Farrell thought for
the thousandth time, more like a retired cook than like the
veteran commander of a Terran Colonies expedition.

Gibson followed, stretching his powerfully-muscled body
like a wrestler to throw off the effects of sleep. Gibson was

linguist-ethnologist of the crew, a blocky man in his early thirties with thick black hair and heavy brows that shaded a square, humorless face.

"Any sign of the squids yet?" he asked.

"They won't show up until the dragons come," Farrell said. He adjusted the light filter of the magnoscanner and scowled at Stryker. "Lee, I wish you'd let me break up the show this time with a dis-beam. This butchery gets on my nerves."

Stryker shielded his eyes with his hands against the glare of sun on water. "You know I can't do that, Arthur. These Arzians may turn out to be Fifth Order beings or higher, and under Terran Regulations our tampering with what may be a basic culture-pattern would amount to armed invasion. We'll have to crack that cackle-and-grunt language of theirs and learn something of their mores before we can interfere."

Farrell turned an irritable stare on the incurious group of Arzians gathering, nets and fishing spears in hand, at the edge of the sheltering bramble forest.

"What stumps me is their motivation," he said. "Why do the fools go out to that islet every night, when they must know damned well what will happen next morning?"

Gibson answered him with an older problem, his square face puzzled. "For that matter, what became of the city I saw when we came in through the stratosphere? It must be a tremendous thing, yet we've searched the entire globe in the scouter and found nothing but water and a scattering of little islands like this one, all covered with bramble. It wasn't a city these pink fishers could have built, either. The architecture was beyond them by a million years."

Stryker and Farrell traded baffled looks. The city had become something of a fixation with Gibson, and his dogged insistence —coupled with an irritating habit of being right—had worn their patience thin.

"There never was a city here, Gib," Stryker said. "You dozed off while we were making planetfall, that's all."

Gibson stiffened resentfully, but Farrell's voice cut his protest short. "Get set! Here they come!"

Out of the morning rainbow dropped a swarm of winged lizards, twenty feet in length and a glistening chlorophyll green in the early light. They swooped like hawks upon the islet off-shore, burying the two Arzian fishers instantly under their snapping, threshing bodies. Then around the outcrop the sea boiled whitely, churned to foam by a sudden uprushing of black, octopoid shapes.

"The squids," Stryker grunted. "Right on schedule. Two seconds too late, as usual, to stop the slaughter."

A barrage of barbed tentacles lashed out of the foam and drove into the melee of winged lizards. The lizards took to the air at once, leaving behind three of their number who disappeared under the surface like harpooned seals. No trace remained of the two Arzian natives.

"A neat example of dog eat dog," Farrell said, snapping off the magnoscanner. "Do any of those beauties look like city-builders, Gib?"

Chattering pink natives straggled past from the shelter of the thorn forest, ignoring the Earthmen, and lined the casting ledges along the beach to begin their day's fishing.

"Nothing we've seen yet could have built that city," Gibson said stubbornly. "But it's here somewhere, and I'm going to find it. Will either of you be using the scouter today?"

Stryker threw up his hands. "I've a mountain of data to collate, and Arthur is off duty after standing watch last night. Help yourself, but you won't find anything."

The scouter was a speeding dot on the horizon when Farrell crawled into his sleeping cubicle a short time later, leaving Stryker to mutter over his litter of notes. Sleep did not come to him at once; a vague sense of something overlooked prodded irritatingly at the back of his consciousness, but it was not until drowsiness had finally overtaken him that the discrepancy assumed definite form.

He recalled then that on the first day of the *Marco's* planet-fall one of the pink fishers had fallen from a casting ledge into the water, and had all but drowned before his fellows pulled him out with extended spear-shafts. Which meant that the fishers could not swim, else some would surely have gone in after him.

And the *Marco's* crew had explored Arz exhaustively without finding any slightest trace of boats or of boat landings. The train of association completed itself with automatic logic, almost rousing Farrell out of his doze.

"I'll be damned," he muttered. "No boats, and they don't swim. *Then how the devil do they get out to that islet?*"

He fell asleep with the paradox unresolved.

Stryker was still humped over his records when Farrell came out of his cubicle and broke a packaged meal from the food locker. The visicom over the control board hummed softly, its screen blank on open channel.

"Gibson found his lost city yet?" Farrell asked, and grinned when Stryker snorted.

"He's scouring the daylight side now," Stryker said. "Arthur, I'm going to ground Gib tomorrow, much as I dislike giving him a direct order. He's got that phantom city on the brain, and he lacks the imagination to understand how dangerous to our assignment an obsession of that sort can be."

Farrell shrugged. "I'd agree with you offhand if it weren't for Gib's bullheaded habit of being right. I hope he finds it soon, if it's here. I'll probably be standing his watch until he's satisfied."

Stryker looked relieved. "Would you mind taking it tonight? I'm completely bushed after today's logging."

Farrell waved a hand and took up his magnoscanner. It was dark outside already, the close, soft night of a moonless tropical world whose moist atmosphere absorbed even starlight. He dragged a chair to the open port and packed his pipe, settling himself comfortably while Stryker mixed a nightcap before turning in.

Later he remembered that Stryker dissolved a tablet in his glass, but at the moment it meant nothing. In a matter of minutes the older man's snoring drifted to him, a sound faintly irritating against the velvety hush outside.

Farrell lit his pipe and turned to the inconsistencies he had uncovered. The Arzians did not swim, and without boats . . .

It occurred to him then that there had been two of the pink fishers on the islet each morning, and the coincidence made him sit up suddenly, startled. Why two? Why not three or four, or only one?

He stepped out through the open lock and paced restlessly up and down on the springy turf, feeling the ocean breeze soft on his face. Three days of dull routine logwork had built up a need for physical action that chafed his temper; he was intrigued and at the same time annoyed by the enigmatic relation that linked the Arzian fishers to the dragons and squids, and his desire to understand that relation was aggravated by the knowledge that Arz could be a perfect world for Terran colonization. That is, he thought wryly, if Terran colonists could stomach the weird custom pursued by its natives of committing suicide in pairs.

He went over again the improbable drama of the past three mornings, and found it not too unnatural until he came to the motivation and the means of transportation that placed the Arzians in pairs on the islet, when his whole fabric of speculation fell into a tangled snarl of inconsistencies. He gave it up finally; how could any Earthman rationalize the outlandish compulsions that actuated so alien a race?

He went inside again, and the sound of Stryker's muffled snoring fanned his restlessness. He made his decision abruptly, laying aside the magnoscanner for a hand-flash and a pocket-sized audicom unit which he clipped to the belt of his shorts.

He did not choose a weapon because he saw no need for one. The torch would show him how the natives reached the outcrop, and if he should need help the audicom would summon Stryker. Investigating without Stryker's sanction was, strictly speaking, a breach of Terran Regulations, but—

"Damn Terran Regulations," he muttered. "I've got to know."

Farrell snapped on the torch at the edge of the thorn forest and entered briskly, eager for action now that he had begun. Just inside the edge of the bramble he came upon a pair of Arzians curled up together on the mossy ground, sleeping soundly, their triangular faces wholly blank and unrevealing.

He worked deeper into the underbrush and found other

sleeping couples, but nothing else. There were no humming insects, no twittering night-birds or scurrying rodents. He had worked his way close to the center of the island without further discovery and was on the point of turning back, disgusted, when something bulky and powerful seized him from behind.

A sharp sting burned his shoulder, wasp-like, and a sudden overwhelming lassitude swept him into a darkness deeper than the Arzian night. His last conscious thought was not of his own danger, but of Stryker—asleep and unprotected behind the *Marco's* open port. . . .

He was standing erect when he woke, his back to the open sea and a prismatic glimmer of early-dawn rainbow shining on the water before him. For a moment he was totally disoriented; then from the corner of an eye he caught the pinkish blur of an Arzian fisher standing beside him, and cried out hoarsely in sudden panic when he tried to turn his head and could not.

He was on the coral outcropping offshore, and except for the involuntary muscles of balance and respiration his body was paralyzed.

The first red glow of sunrise blurred the reflected rainbow at his feet, but for some seconds his shuttling mind was too busy to consider the danger of predicament. *Whatever brought me here anesthetized me first,* he thought. *That sting in my shoulder was like a hypo needle.*

Panic seized him again when he remembered the green flying-lizards; more seconds passed before he gained control of himself, sweating with the effort. He had to get help. If he could switch on the audicom at his belt and call Stryker . . .

He bent every ounce of his will toward raising his right hand, and failed.

His arm was like a limb of lead, its inertia too great to budge. He relaxed the effort with a groan, sweating again when he saw a fiery half-disk of sun on the water, edges blurred and distorted by tiny surface ripples.

On shore he could see the *Marco Four* resting between thorn forest and beach, its silvered sides glistening with dew. The port was still open, and the empty carrier rack in the bow told him that Gibson had not yet returned with the scouter.

He grew aware then that sensation was returning to him slowly, that the cold surface of the audicom unit at his hip—unfelt before—was pressing against the inner curve of his elbow. He bent his will again toward motion; this time the arm tensed a little, enough to send hope flaring through him. If he could put pressure enough against the stud . . .

The tiny click of its engaging sent him faint with relief.

"Stryker!" he yelled. "Lee, roll out—*Stryker!*"

The audicom hummed gently, without answer.

He gathered himself for another shout, and recalled with a chill of horror the tablet Stryker had mixed into his nightcap the night before. Worn out by his work, Stryker had made certain that he would not be easily disturbed.

The flattened sun-disk on the water brightened and grew rounder. Above its reflected glare he caught a flicker of movement, a restless suggestion of flapping wings.

He tried again. "Stryker, help me! I'm on the islet!"

The audicom crackled. The voice that answered was not Stryker's, but Gibson's.

"Farrell! What the devil are you doing on that butcher's block?"

Farrell fought down an insane desire to laugh. "Never mind that—get here fast, Gib! The flying-lizards—"

He broke off, seeing for the first time the octopods that ringed the outcrop just under the surface of the water, waiting with barbed tentacles spread and yellow eyes studying him glassily. He heard the unmistakable flapping of wings behind and above him, and he thought with shock-born lucidity: *I wanted a backstage look at this show, and now I'm one of the cast.*

The scouter roared in from the west across the thorn forest, flashing so close above his head that he felt the wind of its passage. Almost instantly he heard the shrilling blast of its emergency bow jets as Gibson met the lizard swarm head on.

Gibson's voice came tinnily from the audicom. "Scattered them for the moment, Arthur—blinded the whole crew with the exhaust, I think. Stand fast, now. I'm going to pick you up."

The scouter settled on the outcrop beside Farrell, so close

that the hot wash of its exhaust gases scorched his bare legs. Gibson put out thick brown arms and hauled him inside like a straw man, ignoring the native. The scouter darted for shore with Farrell lying across Gibson's knees in the cockpit, his head hanging half overside.

Farrell had a last dizzy glimpse of the islet against the rush of green water below, and felt his shaky laugh of relief stick in his throat. Two of the octopods were swimming strongly for shore, holding the rigid Arzian native carefully above water between them.

"Gib," Farrell croaked. "Gib, can you risk a look back? I think I've gone mad."

The scouter swerved briefly as Gibson looked back. "You're all right, Arthur. Just hang on tight. I'll explain everything when we get you safe in the *Marco*."

Farrell forced himself to relax, more relieved than alarmed by the painful pricking of returning sensation. "I might have known it, damn you," he said. "You found your lost city, didn't you?"

Gibson sounded a little disgusted, as if he were still angry with himself over some private stupidity. "I'd have found it sooner if I'd had any brains. It was under water, of course."

In the *Marco Four*, Gibson routed Stryker out of his cubicle and mixed drinks around, leaving Farrell comfortably relaxed in the padded control chair. The paralysis was still wearing off slowly, easing Farrell's fear of being permanently disabled.

"We never saw the city from the scouter because we didn't go high enough," Gibson said. "I realized that finally, remembering how they used high-altitude blimps during the First Wars to spot submarines, and when I took the scouter up far enough there it was, at the ocean bottom—a city to compare with anything men ever built."

Stryker stared. "A marine city? What use would sea-creatures have for buildings?"

"None," Gibson said. "I think the city must have been built ages ago—by men or by a manlike race, judging from the architecture—and was submerged later by a sinking of land masses that killed off the original builders and left Arz nothing but an oversized archipelago. The squids took over then, and from all appearances they've developed a culture of their own."

"I don't see it," Stryker complained, shaking his head. "The pink fishers—"

"Are cattle, or less," Gibson finished. "The octopods are the dominant race, and they're so far above Fifth Order that we're completely out of bounds here. Under Terran Regulations we can't colonize Arz. It would be armed invasion."

"Invasion of a squid world?" Farrell protested, baffled. "Why should surface colonization conflict with an undersea culture, Gib? Why couldn't we share the planet?"

"Because the octopods own the islands too, and keep them policed," Gibson said patiently. "They even own the pink fishers. It was one of the squid-people, making a dry-land canvass of his preserve here to pick a couple of victims for this morning's show, that carried you off last night."

"Behold a familiar pattern shaping up," Stryker said. He laughed suddenly, a great irrepressible bellow of sound. "Arz is a squid's world, Arthur, don't you see? And like most civilized peoples, they're sportsmen. The flying-lizards are the game they hunt, and they raise the pink fishers for—"

Farrell swore in astonishment. "Then those poor devils are put out there deliberately, like worms on a hook—angling in reverse! No wonder I couldn't spot their motivation!"

Gibson got up and sealed the port, shutting out the soft morning breeze. "Colonization being out of the question, we may as well move on before the octopods get curious enough about us to make trouble. Do you feel up to the acceleration, Arthur?"

Farrell and Stryker looked at each other, grinning. Farrell said: "You don't think I want to stick here and be used for bait again, do you?"

He and Stryker were still grinning over it when Gibson, unamused, blasted the *Marco Four* free of Arz.

THE GAME OF RAT AND DRAGON
by Cordwainer Smith

*Cats today are among the most popular pets.
Indeed, it is said that whenever a picture of a cat
appears on a magazine cover, sales of that
magazine increase. But times change, and it is
possible that in a future world, humans and
cats will have an even more interdependent
relationship.*

Pinlighting is a heck of a way to earn a living. Underhill was furious as he closed the door behind himself. It didn't make much sense to wear a uniform and look like a soldier if people didn't appreciate what you did.

He sat down in his chair, laid his head back in the head-rest and pulled the helmet down over his forehead.

As he waited for the pin-set to warm up, he remembered the girl in the outer corridor. She had looked at it, then looked at him scornfully.

"Meow." That was all she had said. Yet it had cut him like a knife.

What did she think he was—a fool, a loafer, a uniformed nonentity? Didn't she know that for every half hour of pinlighting, he got a minimum of two months' recuperation in the hospital?

By now the set was warm. He felt the squares of space around him, sensed himself at the middle of an immense grid, a cubic grid, full of nothing. Out in that nothingness, he could sense the hollow aching horror of space itself and could feel the terrible anxiety which his mind encountered whenever it met the faintest trace of inert dust.

As he relaxed, the comforting solidity of the Sun, the

clockwork of the familiar planets and the Moon rang in on him. Our own solar system was as charming and as simple as an ancient cuckoo clock filled with familiar ticking and with reassuring noises. The odd little moons of Mars swung around their planet like frantic mice, yet their regularity was itself an assurance that all was well. Far above the plane of the ecliptic, he could feel half a ton of dust more or less drifting outside the lanes of human travel.

Here there was nothing to fight, nothing to challenge the mind, to tear the living soul out of a body with its roots dripping in effluvium as tangible as blood.

Nothing ever moved in on the Solar System. He could wear the pin-set forever and be nothing more than a sort of telepathic astronomer, a man who could feel the hot, warm protection of the Sun throbbing and burning against his living mind.

Woodley came in.

"Same old ticking world," said Underhill. "Nothing to report. No wonder they didn't develop the pin-set until they began to planoform. Down here with the hot Sun around us, it feels so good and so quiet. You can feel everything spinning and turning. It's nice and sharp and compact. It's sort of like sitting around home."

Woodley grunted. He was not much given to flights of fantasy.

Undeterred, Underhill went on, "It must have been pretty good to have been an ancient man. I wonder why they burned up their world with war. They didn't have to planoform. They didn't have to go out to earn their livings among the stars. They didn't have to dodge the Rats or play the Game. They couldn't have invented pinlighting because they didn't have any need of it, did they, Woodley?"

Woodley grunted, "Uh-huh." Woodley was twenty-six years old and due to retire in one more year. He already had a farm picked out. He had gotten through ten years of hard work pinlighting with the best of them. He had kept his sanity by not thinking very much about his job, meeting the strains of the task whenever he had to meet them and thinking nothing more about his duties until the next emergency arose.

Woodley never made a point of getting popular among the Partners. None of the Partners liked him very much. Some of them even resented him. He was suspected of thinking ugly thoughts of the Partners on occasion, but since none of the Partners ever thought a complaint in articulate form, the other pinlighters and the Chiefs of the Instrumentality left him alone.

Underhill was still full of the wonder of his job. Happily he babbled on, "What does happen to us when we planoform? Do you think it's sort of like dying? Did you ever see anybody who had his soul pulled out?"

"Pulling souls is just a way of talking about it," said Woodley. "After all these years, nobody knows whether we have souls or not."

"But I saw one once. I saw what Dogwood looked like when he came apart. There was something funny. It looked wet and sort of sticky as if it were bleeding and it went out of him—and you know what they did to Dogwood? They took him away, up in that part of the hospital where you and I never go—way up at the top part where the others are, where the others always have to go if they are alive after the Rats of the Up-and-Out have gotten them."

Woodley sat down and lit an ancient pipe. He was burning something called tobacco in it. It was a dirty sort of habit, but it made him look very dashing and adventurous.

"Look here, youngster. You don't have to worry about that stuff. Pinlighting is getting better all the time. The Partners are getting better. I've seen them pinlight two Rats forty-six million miles apart in one and a half milliseconds. As long as people had to try to work the pin-sets themselves, there was always the chance that with a minimum of four hundred milliseconds for the human mind to set a pinlight, we wouldn't light the Rats up fast enough to protect our planoforming ships. The Partners have changed all that. Once they get going, they're faster than Rats. And they always will be. I know it's not easy, letting a Partner share your mind—"

"It's not easy for them, either," said Underhill.

"Don't worry about them. They're not human. Let them take care of themselves. I've seen more pinlighters go crazy from monkeying around with Partners than I have ever seen caught by the Rats. How many do you actually know of them that got grabbed by Rats?"

Underhill looked down at his fingers, which shone green and purple in the vivid light thrown by the tuned-in pin-set, and counted ships. The thumb for the *Andromeda,* lost with crew and passengers, the index finger and the middle finger for *Release Ships* 43 and 56, found with their pin-sets burned out and every man, woman, and child on board dead or insane. The ring finger, the little finger, and the thumb of the other hand were the first three battleships to be lost to the Rats—lost as people realized that there was something out there *underneath space itself* which was alive, capricious and malevolent.

Planoforming was sort of funny. It felt like—

Like nothing much.

Like the twinge of a mild electric shock.

Like the ache of a sore tooth bitten on for the first time.

Like a slightly painful flash of light against the eyes.

Yet in that time, a forty-thousand-ton ship lifting free above Earth disappeared somehow or other into two dimensions and appeared half a light-year or fifty light-years off.

At one moment, he would be sitting in the Fighting Room, the pin-set ready and the familiar Solar System ticking around inside his head. For a second or a year (he could never tell how long it really was, subjectively), the funny little flash went through him and then he was loose in the Up-and-Out, the terrible open spaces between the stars, where the stars themselves felt like pimples on his telepathic mind and the planets were too far away to be sensed or read.

Somewhere in this outer space, a gruesome death awaited, death and horror of a kind which Man had never encountered until he reached out for interstellar space itself. Apparently the light of the suns kept the Dragons away.

Dragons. That was what people called them. To ordinary people, there was nothing, nothing except the shiver of planoforming and the hammer blow of sudden death or the dark spastic note of lunacy descending into their minds.

But to the telepaths, they were Dragons.

In the fraction of a second between the telepaths' awareness of a hostile something out in the black, hollow nothingness of space and the impact of a ferocious, ruinous psychic blow against all living things within the ship, the telepaths had sensed entities something like the Dragons of ancient human lore, beasts more clever than beasts, demons more tangible than demons, hungry vortices of aliveness and hate compounded by unknown means out of the thin tenuous matter between the stars.

It took a surviving ship to bring back the news—a ship in which, by sheer chance, a telepath had a light beam ready, turning it out at the innocent dust so that, within the panorama of his mind, the Dragon dissolved into nothing at all and the other passengers, themselves non-telepathic, went about their way not realizing that their own immediate deaths had been averted.

From then on, it was easy—almost.

Planoforming ships always carried telepaths. Telepaths had their sensitiveness enlarged to an immense range by the pin-sets, which were telepathic amplifiers adapted to the mammal mind. The pin-sets in turn were electronically geared into small dirigible light bombs. Light did it.

Light broke up the Dragons, allowed the ships to reform three-dimensionally, skip, skip, skip, as they moved from star to star.

The odds suddenly moved down from a hundred to one against mankind to sixty to forty in mankind's favor.

This was not enough. The telepaths were trained to become ultrasensitive, trained to become aware of the Dragons in less than a millisecond.

But it was found that the Dragons could move a million miles in just under two milliseconds and that this was not enough for the human mind to activate the light beams.

Attempts had been made to sheath the ships in light at all times.

This defense wore out.

As mankind learned about the Dragons, so too, apparently, the Dragons learned about mankind. Somehow they flattened their own bulk and came in on extremely flat trajectories very quickly.

Intense light was needed, light of sunlike intensity. This could be provided only by light bombs. Pinlighting came into existence.

Pinlighting consisted of the detonation of ultravivid miniature photonuclear bombs, which converted a few ounces of a magnesium isotope into pure visible radiance.

The odds kept coming down in mankind's favor, yet ships were being lost.

It became so bad that people didn't even want to find the ships because the rescuers knew what they would see. It was sad to bring back to Earth three hundred bodies ready for burial and two hundred or three hundred lunatics, damaged beyond repair, to be wakened, and fed, and cleaned, and put to sleep, wakened and fed again until their lives were ended.

Telepaths tried to reach into the minds of the psychotics who had been damaged by the Dragons, but they found nothing there beyond vivid spouting columns of fiery terror bursting from the primordial id itself, the volcanic source of life.

Then came the Partners.

Man and Partner could do together what Man could not do alone. Men had the intellect. Partners had the speed.

The Partners rode their tiny craft, no larger than footballs, outside the spaceships. They planoformed with the ships. They rode beside them in their six-pound craft ready to attack.

The tiny ships of the Partners were swift. Each carried a dozen pinlights, bombs no bigger than thimbles.

The pinlighters threw the Partners—quite literally threw—by means of mind-to-firing relays direct at the Dragons.

What seemed to be Dragons to the human mind appeared in the form of gigantic Rats in the minds of the Partners.

Out in the pitiless nothingness of space, the Partners' minds responded to an instinct as old as life. The Partners attacked, striking with a speed faster than Man's, going from attack to attack until the Rats or themselves were destroyed. Almost all the time, it was the Partners who won.

With the safety of the interstellar skip, skip, skip of the ships, commerce increased immensely, the population of all the colonies went up, and the demand for trained Partners increased.

Underhill and Woodley were a part of the third generation of pinlighters and yet, to them, it seemed as though their craft had endured forever.

Gearing space into minds by means of the pin-set, adding the Partners to those minds, keying up the mind for the tension of a fight on which all depended—this was more than human synapses could stand for long. Underhill needed his two months' rest after half an hour of fighting. Woodley needed his retirement after ten years of service. They were young. They were good. But they had limitations.

So much depended on the choice of Partners, so much on the sheer luck of who drew whom.

Father Moontree and the little girl named West entered the room. They were the other two pinlighters. The human complement of the Fighting Room was now complete.

Father Moontree was a red-faced man of forty-five who had lived the peaceful life of a farmer until he reached his fortieth year. Only then, belatedly, did the authorities find he was telepathic and agree to let him late in life enter upon the career of pinlighter. He did well at it, but he was fantastically old for this kind of business.

Father Moontree looked at the glum Woodley and the musing Underhill. "How're the youngsters today? Ready for a good fight?"

"Father always wants a fight," giggled the little girl named West. She was such a little little girl. Her giggle was high and childish. She looked like the last person in the world one would expect to find in the rough, sharp dueling of pinlighting.

Underhill had been amused one time when he found one of the most sluggish of the Partners coming away happy from contact with the mind of the girl named West.

Usually the Partners didn't care much about the human minds with which they were paired for the journey. The Partners seemed to take the attitude that human minds were complex and fouled up beyond belief, anyhow. No Partner ever questioned the superiority of the human mind, though very few of the Partners were much impressed by that superiority.

The Partners liked people. They were willing to fight with them. They were even willing to die for them. But when a Partner liked an individual the way, for example, that Captain Wow or the Lady May liked Underhill, the liking had nothing to do with intellect. It was a matter of temperament, of feel.

Underhill knew perfectly well that Captain Wow regarded his, Underhill's, brains as silly. What Captain Wow liked was Underhill's friendly emotional structure, the cheerfulness and glint of wicked amusement that shot through Underhill's unconscious thought patterns, and the gaiety with which Underhill faced danger. The words, the history books, the ideas, the science —Underhill could sense all that in his own mind, reflected back from Captain Wow's mind, as so much rubbish.

Miss West looked at Underhill. "I bet you've put stickum on the stones."

"I did not!"

Underhill felt his ears grow red with embarrassment. During his novitiate, he had tried to cheat in the lottery because he got particularly fond of a special Partner, a lovely young mother named Murr. It was so much easier to operate with Murr and she was so affectionate toward him that he forgot pinlighting was hard work and that he was not instructed to have a good time with his Partner. They were both designed and prepared to go into deadly battle together.

One cheating had been enough. They had found him out and he had been laughed at for years.

Father Moontree picked up the imitation-leather cup and shook the stone dice which assigned them their Partners for the trip. By senior rights, he took first draw.

He grimaced. He had drawn a greedy old character, a tough old male whose mind was full of slobbering thoughts of food, veritable oceans full of half-spoiled fish. Father Moontree had once said that he burped cod-liver oil for weeks after drawing that particular glutton, so strongly had the telepathic image of fish impressed itself upon his mind. Yet the glutton was a glutton for danger as well as for fish. He had killed sixty-three

Dragons, more than any other Partner in the service, and was quite literally worth his weight in gold.

The little girl West came next. She drew Captain Wow. When she saw who it was, she smiled.

"I *like* him," she said. "He's such fun to fight with. He feels so nice and cuddly in my mind."

"Cuddly?" said Woodley. "I've been in his mind, too. It's the most leering mind in this ship, bar none."

"Nasty man," said the little girl. She said it declaratively, without reproach.

Underhill, looking at her, shivered.

He didn't see how she could take Captain Wow so calmly. Captain Wow's mind *did* leer. When Captain Wow got excited in the middle of a battle, confused images of Dragons, deadly Rats, luscious beds, the smell of fish, and the shock of space all scrambled together in his mind as he and Captain Wow, their consciousnesses linked together through the pin-set, became a fantastic composite of human being and Persian cat.

That's the trouble with working with cats, thought Underhill. It's a pity that nothing else anywhere will serve as Partner. Cats were all right once you got in touch with them telepathically. They were smart enough to meet the needs of the fight, but their motives and desires were certainly different from those of humans.

They were companionable enough as long as you thought tangible images at them, but their minds just closed up and went to sleep when you recited Shakespeare or Colegrove, or if you tried to tell them what space was.

It was sort of funny realizing that the Partners who were so grim and mature out here in space were the same cute little animals that people had used as pets for thousands of years back on Earth. He had embarrassed himself more than once while on the ground saluting perfectly ordinary non-telepathic cats because he had forgotten for the moment that they were not Partners.

He picked up the cup and shook out his stone dice.

He was lucky—he drew the Lady May.

The Lady May was the most thoughtful Partner he had

ever met. In her, the finely bred pedigree mind of a Persian cat had reached one of its highest peaks of development. She was more complex than any human woman, but the complexity was all one of emotions, memory, hope and discriminated experience—experience sorted through without benefit of words.

When he had first come into contact with her mind, he was astonished at its clarity. With her he remembered her kittenhood. He remembered every mating experience she had ever had. He saw in a half-recognizable gallery all the other pinlighters with whom she had been paired for the fight. And he saw himself radiant, cheerful and desirable.

He even thought he caught the edge of a longing—

A very flattering and yearning thought: *What a pity he is not a cat.*

Woodley picked up the last stone. He drew what he deserved—a sullen, scared old tomcat with none of the verve of Captain Wow. Woodley's Partner was the most animal of all the cats on the ship, a low, brutish type with a dull mind. Even telepathy had not refined his character. His ears were half chewed off from the first fights in which he had engaged.

He was a serviceable fighter, nothing more.

Woodley grunted.

Underhill glanced at him oddly. Didn't Woodley ever do anything but grunt?

Father Moontree looked at the other three. "You might as well get your Partners now. I'll let the Scanner know we're ready to go into the Up-and-Out."

Underhill spun the combination lock on the Lady May's cage. He woke her gently and took her into his arms. She humped her back luxuriously, stretched her claws, started to purr, thought better of it, and licked him on the wrist instead. He did not have the pin-set on, so their minds were closed to each other, but in the angle of her mustache and in the movement of her ears, he caught some sense of gratification she experienced in finding him as her Partner.

He talked to her in human speech, even though speech meant nothing to a cat when the pin-set was not on.

"It's a damn shame, sending a sweet little thing like you

whirling around in the coldness of nothing to hunt for Rats that are bigger and deadlier than all of us put together. You didn't ask for this kind of fight, did you?"

For answer, she licked his hand, purred, tickled his cheek with her long fluffy tail, turned around and faced him, golden eyes shining.

For a moment, they stared at each other, man squatting, cat standing erect on her hind legs, front claws digging into his knee. Human eyes and cat eyes looked across an immensity which no words could meet, but which affection spanned in a single glance.

"Time to get in," he said.

She walked docilely into her spheroid carrier. She climbed in. He saw to it that her miniature pin-set rested firmly and comfortably against the base of her brain. He made sure that her claws were padded so that she could not tear herself in the excitement of battle.

Softly he said to her, "Ready?"

For answer, she preened her back as much as her harness would permit and purred softly within the confines of the frame that held her.

He slapped down the lid and watched the sealant ooze around the seam. For a few hours, she was welded into her projectile until a workman with a short cutting arc would remove her after she had done her duty.

He picked up the entire projectile and slipped it into the ejection tube. He closed the door of the tube, spun the lock, seated himself in his chair, and put his own pin-set on.

Once again he flung the switch.

He sat in a small room, *small, small, warm, warm,* the bodies of the other three people moving close around him, the tangible lights in the ceiling bright and heavy against his closed eyelids.

As the pin-set warmed, the room fell away. The other people ceased to be people and became small glowing heaps of fire, embers, dark red fire, with the consciousness of life burning like old red coals in a country fireplace.

As the pin-set warmed a little more, he felt Earth just below him, felt the ship slipping away, felt the turning Moon as it swung on the far side of the world, felt the planets and the hot, clear goodness of the Sun which kept the Dragons so far from mankind's native ground.

Finally, he reached complete awareness.

He was telepathically alive to a range of millions of miles. He felt the dust which he had noticed earlier high above the ecliptic. With a thrill of warmth and tenderness, he felt the consciousness of the Lady May pouring over into his own. Her consciousness was as gentle and clear and yet sharp to the taste of his mind as if it were scented oil. It felt relaxing and reassuring. He could sense her welcome of him. It was scarcely a thought, just a raw emotion of greeting.

At last they were one again.

In a tiny remote corner of his mind, as tiny as the smallest toy he had ever seen in his childhood, he was still aware of the room and the ship, and of Father Moontree picking up a telephone and speaking to a Scanner captain in charge of the ship.

His telepathic mind caught the idea long before his ears could frame the words. The actual sound followed the idea the way that thunder on an ocean beach follows the lightning inward from far out over the seas.

"The Fighting Room is ready. Clear to planoform, sir."

Underhill was always a little exasperated the way that Lady May experienced things before he did.

He was braced for the quick vinegar thrill of planoforming, but he caught her report of it before his own nerves could register what happened.

Earth had fallen so far away that he groped for several milliseconds before he found the Sun in the upper rear right-hand corner of his telepathic mind.

That was a good jump, he thought. This way we'll get there in four or five skips.

A few hundred miles outside the ship, the Lady May thought back at him, "O warm, O generous, O gigantic man! O brave, O friendly, O tender and huge Partner! O wonderful with you, with you so good, good, good, warm, warm, now to fight, now to go, good with you . . ."

He knew that she was not thinking words, that his mind took the clear amiable babble of her cat intellect and translated it into images which his own thinking could record and understand.

Neither one of them was absorbed in the game of mutual greetings. He reached out far beyond her range of perception to see if there was anything near the ship. It was funny how it was possible to do two things at once. He could scan space with his pin-set mind and yet at the same time catch a vagrant thought of hers, a lovely, affectionate thought about a son who had had a golden face and a chest covered with soft, incredibly downy white fur.

While he was still searching, he caught the warning from her.

We jump again!

And so they had. The ship had moved to a second planoform. The stars were different. The sun was immeasurably far behind. Even the nearest stars were barely in contact. This was good Dragon country, this open, nasty, hollow kind of space. He reached farther, faster, sensing and looking for danger, ready to fling the Lady May at danger wherever he found it.

Terror blazed up in his mind, so sharp, so clear, that it came through as a physical wrench.

The little girl named West had found something—something immense, long, black, sharp, greedy, horrific. She flung Captain Wow at it.

Underhill tried to keep his own mind clear. "Watch out!" he shouted telepathically at the others, trying to move the Lady May around.

At one corner of the battle, he felt the lustful rage of Captain Wow as the big Persian tomcat detonated lights while he approached the streak of dust which threatened the ship and the people within.

The lights scored near-misses.

The dust flattened itself, changing from the shape of a sting-ray into the shape of a spear.

Not three milliseconds had elapsed.

Father Moontree was talking human words and was saying in a voice that moved like cold molasses out of a heavy jar,

"C-a-p-t-a-i-n." Underhill knew that the sentence was going to be "Captain, move fast!"

The battle would be fought and finished before Father Moontree got through talking.

Now, fractions of a millisecond later, the Lady May was directly in line.

Here was where the skill and speed of the Partners came in. She could react faster than he. She could see the threat as an immense Rat coming direct at her.

She could fire the light bombs with a discrimination which he might miss.

He was connected with her mind, but he could not follow it.

His consciousness absorbed the tearing wound inflicted by the alien enemy. It was like no wound on Earth—raw, crazy pain which started like a burn at his navel. He began to writhe in his chair.

Actually he had not yet had time to move a muscle when the Lady May struck back at their enemy.

Five evenly spaced photonuclear bombs blazed out across a hundred thousand miles.

The pain in his mind and body vanished.

He felt a moment of fierce, terrible, feral elation running through the mind of the Lady May as she finished her kill. It was always disappointing to the cats to find out that their enemies whom they sensed as gigantic space Rats disappeared at the moment of destruction.

Then he felt her hurt, the pain and the fear that swept over both of them as the battle, quicker than the movement of an eyelid, had come and gone. In the same instant, there came the sharp and acid twinge of planoform.

Once more the ship went skip.

He could hear Woodley thinking at him. "You don't have to bother much. This old son of a gun and I will take over for a while."

Twice again the twinge, the skip.

He had no idea where he was until the lights of the Caledonia space board shone below.

With a weariness that lay almost beyond the limits of thought, he threw his mind back into rapport with the pin-set, fixing the Lady May's projectile gently and neatly in its launching tube.

She was half dead with fatigue, but he could feel the beat of her heart, could listen to her panting, and he grasped the grateful edge of a thanks reaching from her mind to his.

They put him in the hospital at Caledonia.

The doctor was friendly but firm. "You actually got touched by that Dragon. That's as close a shave as I've ever seen. It's all so quick that it'll be a long time before we know what happened scientifically, but I suppose you'd be ready for the insane asylum now if the contact had lasted several tenths of a millisecond longer. What kind of cat did you have out in front of you?"

Underhill felt the words coming out of him slowly. Words were such a lot of trouble compared with the speed and the joy of thinking, fast and sharp and clear, mind to mind! But words were all that could reach ordinary people like this doctor.

His mouth moved heavily as he articulated words, "Don't call our Partners cats. The right thing to call them is Partners. They fight for us in a team. You ought to know we call them Partners, not cats. How is mine?"

"I don't know," said the doctor contritely. "We'll find out for you. Meanwhile, old man, you take it easy. There's nothing but rest that can help you. Can you make yourself sleep, or would you like us to give you some kind of sedative?"

"I can sleep," said Underhill. "I just want to know about the Lady May."

The nurse joined in. She was a little antagonistic. "Don't you want to know about the other people?"

"They're okay," said Underhill. "I knew that before I came in here."

He stretched his arms and sighed and grinned at them. He could see they were relaxing and were beginning to treat him as a person instead of a patient.

"I'm all right," he said. "Just let me know when I can go see my Partner."

A new thought struck him. He looked wildly at the doctor. "They didn't send her off with the ship, did they?"

"I'll find out right away," said the doctor. He gave Underhill a reassuring squeeze of the shoulder and left the room.

The nurse took a napkin off a goblet of chilled fruit juice.

Underhill tried to smile at her. There seemed to be something wrong with the girl. He wished she would go away. First she had started to be friendly and now she was distant again. It's a nuisance being telepathic, he thought. You keep trying to reach even when you are not making contact.

Suddenly she swung around on him.

"You pinlighters! You and your damn cats!"

Just as she stamped out, he burst into her mind. He saw himself a radiant hero, clad in his smooth suede uniform, the pin-set crown shining like ancient royal jewels around his head. He saw his own face, handsome and masculine, shining out of her mind. He saw himself very far away and he saw himself as she hated him.

She hated him in the secrecy of her own mind. She hated him because he was—she thought—proud, and strange, and rich, better and more beautiful than people like her.

He cut off the sight of her mind and, as he buried his face in the pillow, he caught an image of the Lady May.

"She *is* a cat," he thought. "That's all she is—a *cat!*"

But that was not how his mind saw her—quick beyond all dreams of speed, sharp, clever, unbelievably graceful, beautiful, wordless and undemanding.

Where would he ever find a woman who could compare with her?

DATE DUE			